COURAGE, DANA

COURAGE, DANA

Susan Beth Pfeffer

Illustrated by Jenny Rutherford

A YEARLING BOOK

Published by
Dell Publishing
a division of
The Bantam Doubleday Dell Publishing Group, Inc.
666 Fifth Avenue
New York, New York 10103

ISBN: 0-440-41541-1

Reprinted by arrangement with Delacorte Press
Printed in the United States of America

January 1984

10 9 8

OPM

For my twenty-two aunts and uncles

1

It had been a pretty average day until I became a heroine.

We got back our spelling tests, and I'd gotten an 85, which was a relief, since I hadn't studied for it. I was called on to do a problem in math, and I got it without too much trouble.

Sharon and I had lunch together, along with a couple of the other girls. We talked about some of the shows on TV the night before, and the book reports that were due on Friday. Only Sharon had read her book all the way through. I still had half to go.

We played soccer in gym, and I helped my team get a goal. The day was bright-blue sunny, and it was a drag to have to go back indoors. Social studies was the last thing that day, and mostly I looked out the window and thought about what a good time I'd had during the summer, swimming and hiking, and just messing around.

After school I walked through the playground and saw Charlie Everest teasing Brian O'Shea again. Charlie was the class bully, and he had been since he came to our school in second grade. Brian was new, and I didn't have much of an impression of him yet. He seemed quiet, maybe a little shy. Bright enough, but not so smart you'd notice. He wasn't enough of anything to notice. Unlike Charlie, who had always been at least four inches taller and twenty pounds heavier than any of us. A hundred times meaner, too. Right then he was pushing his index finger into Brian's chest and calling him a sissy and a wimp. Sissy first, then wimp. Brian just stood there, not moving, but not crying either. Charlie usually made kids cry. He'd made me cry more than once in the past five years.

It was mean of me, but I was glad he was picking on somebody else. A boy too. Boys should be able to take care of themselves against other boys, I figured.

"Sissywimp," Charlie said, the two words becoming one as he jabbed away. "Sissywimp."

I think I would have kicked Charlie by then, but Brian didn't do a thing.

"Hey, cut it out," one of the older kids said. Now that we were in junior high, Charlie was no longer the biggest kid in the whole school.

Charlie glared at the boy, but he stopped poking at

Brian. Brian picked up his schoolbooks and started walking away.

"He is a sissywimp," Charlie announced, but he didn't have much of an audience. I heard him mutter "Sissywimp" one last time, and then I crossed the yard and started walking toward home.

"Where are you going?" Sharon asked me. I hadn't noticed her running toward me.

"Home," I said. "Where else?"

"Oh, I don't know," she said, but I could tell from the look in her eyes she was thinking ice cream. Sharon and I have been best friends since kindergarten, and we knew each other's looks pretty well.

"Why not?" I said before she even had a chance to ask. It might be the last warm day until May, and a final farewell-to-summer ice cream cone sounded like a good idea. So we walked the few extra blocks to the Cream King and ordered soft vanilla cones with sprinkles.

"Seventh grade's okay so far," Sharon said between licks. We'd been seventh graders for two weeks already.

"I like being in junior high," I said. "I felt like a baby in elementary school. Especially with Jean in junior high, telling me all the good stuff I was missing."

"Like dances," Sharon said, wiping a spot of ice cream from her jeans. I love Sharon, but she's the world's messiest eater. "I can't wait until the Halloween dance."

"Do you think you'll have a real date?" I asked.

"I'm sure going to try," Sharon said. "Maybe Jean can help us."

"Jean?" I repeated with a laugh. Jean already had a boyfriend, Big Wally, but that didn't mean she passed her rejects along.

"She might," Sharon said.

"Don't count on it," I replied, nibbling at my cone. When it was finished, that meant summer was finished too. Of course summer had officially ended the first day of school, but the end of the ice cream cone meant the end of it all permanently. I felt a little sad thinking of it that way, and considered getting a second cone just to postpone the moment.

"Jean's okay," Sharon said. "She lends you her clothes."

"Jean's fine." I said. "She says just as long as I keep quiet at school, so she doesn't have to tell people she's my sister, we'll get along just fine."

"That's not too much to ask," Sharon said. "Just be invisible for a year."

"Did you see Charlie teasing Brian?" I asked, taking one sorrowful last lick of ice cream.

"Charlie's awful," Sharon said, finishing her cone at the same time. "I wish somebody would finally put him in his place."

"You mean in jail?" I asked, and we both giggled.

"With striped pants," Sharon said. "Like in those old comedies. And handcuffs."

"And people bringing him saws in chocolate cakes," I said, and we started whooping with laughter. It took a moment before Sharon had calmed down enough to wipe the few remaining sprinkles off her shirt.

"Who'd want Charlie to escape?" she asked. "More likely they'll swallow the key and keep him in jail forever."

"You're not fooling me," I said. "I know you have a crush on him. You'd visit him every single weekend and write him love letters and cry all the time he was behind bars."

"If I loved Charlie, you'd better believe I'd be crying," Sharon said. "Poor Brian. Do you think Charlie is going to pick on him all year, like he did to Michael Stevens two years ago?"

I hadn't thought about Michael in a long time, and hearing his name forced all the good feeling out of me. Eventually Michael's parents had taken him out of school and put him into a parochial school, just to keep Charlie away from him.

"They won't let him get away with that sort of stuff here," I said. "Someone'll stop Charlie before it gets that bad."

"It won't be me," Sharon said. "I don't want to get Charlie mad at me."

"Me either," I said. "But I'd really like to hit him sometimes."

"Sure," Sharon said. "But I want to live to see eighth grade. Preferably with a face all in one piece."

"I don't know," I said. "A nose job or two might not hurt."

"Two?" Sharon shrieked. "How many noses do you think I have, Dana? Two? Three? Four?"

"Eighteen," I said, and we were giggling again. "I know where you keep them hidden, Sharon."

"I may have eighteen noses, but at least I have a brain," she said. "Eighteen noses. Honestly, Dana."

"Honestly, Sharon," I said, and it was hard to stand, we were laughing so hard. It wasn't that we were so funny. It was just that it felt so good to be outside on such a beautiful day. Even if there was school the next day and the day after that and after that for the next nine months.

"I gotta go," Sharon finally choked out. "Homework."

"Me too," I said, sobering up fast. "Math and social studies."

"And reading your book for the book report," Sharon said.

"That too," I said, and we turned away from each other, since our homes were in different directions. "Hey, Sharon . . ."

"Yeah?"

"Don't forget to count your noses when you get home. Your mother might have borrowed one."

Sharon snorted and I giggled. I felt really good just then. Maybe things weren't perfect, but as long as the sun was shining and there were still flowers blooming, it was all right.

Like I said, it was a pretty average day.

I got to the corner of Main and North streets, just in time to miss the traffic light. I swear they run that thing just for pedestrians to have to stand there. It's a busy corner, and unless you're really feeling daring, you don't cross against the light. That's the sort of dumb thing Charlie might do, but not me. I wasn't in that big a hurry to get home and work on my book report.

I half noticed the people who were waiting for the light with me, the way you half notice things when you really aren't thinking about anything special, just waiting to cross the street. There was a woman carrying a bag from Woolworth's, and a man in a business suit who looked a little like my father, and a mother with a half dozen packages in one hand, trying to control her little kid with the other. The kid was two or maybe three. I don't have that much experience with little kids, so it's hard for me to tell how old they are, or if they're boys or girls. This one was just a wriggling kid in overalls and a blue shirt.

But then the kid managed to wriggle away from its

mother. And before she even had a chance to notice, the kid had run smack into the middle of Main and North streets, with a big blue car coming right at it.

The funny thing is I didn't even think. If I'd taken one second to think, I never would have moved. I would have stood there frozen and watched the car hit the kid. It couldn't possibly have stopped in time. I couldn't even be sure if the driver would see the kid, it was so little.

Not that any of that really registered. Instead, I ran into the street, right into the path of that big blue car, and pushed the kid out of the way. The momentum of pushing kept me going, and I stumbled along, half holding the hysterical kid and half holding my schoolbooks.

I knew the car could hit us. It was roaring at us like a blue giant. But the funny thing was I felt like a giant too, an all-powerful one, like even if the car hit us, it wouldn't hurt us because I was made of steel, too. Like Superman. And as long as I was there, the kid was safe. I moved my giant steel legs and lifted the kid with my giant steel arms, and in what couldn't have been more than ten seconds, but felt more like ten years, I pushed both of us out of the path of the car.

By the time I'd gotten to the other side of the street with the kid, the blue car's brakes were screeching it to a halt. But over that noise, and the noise of the kid crying, I

could hear its mother screaming from way across the street. It was amazing how far off she looked.

I really wanted to lean against the lamppost, but I wasn't going to let go of that kid. I'd already lost most of my books, since I wasn't about to go to the middle of the street and pick them up where I'd dropped them. So I stood there, holding on to the kid with my grip getting weaker and weaker as I started to realize just what I'd done, and just what the car could have done to the kid and me.

The man in the business suit stood in the middle of the street, holding his hand up to stop the cars, and picked up my books for me. The kid's mother, still screaming, crossed the street, walked over to where we were, and started weeping. She was shaking pretty hard, too, but nowhere near as hard as I was. The kid ran to its mother, and the two of them hugged and sobbed. That left me free to grab onto the lamppost, which I did, with both arms.

"I couldn't see, I didn't see," the driver of the blue car cried at us. I guess she pulled her car over to the side of the street, because I watched her join us. She seemed like a nice lady, too, not the sort that drove blue giant monster cars and aimed them at kids. "I have two of my own. I never would have . . ."

"He just got away from me," the kid's mother said. "I

was holding his hand, and then he just broke away from me. . . ."

"Here are your books," the businessman said, handing them to me. That meant I had to give up the lamppost, which I did reluctantly. That car could have killed me. I risked my life for some little kid—I didn't even know if it was a boy or a girl. I could have been killed trying to save some strange kid's life.

"I have to go home now," I said, trying to sound conversational. Nobody was paying any attention to me anyway. I grabbed my books, and took about a half dozen steps away from the corner of Main and North streets before my legs gave way, and I practically sank onto the sidewalk.

"I'll drive you home," the woman with the Woolworth's bag said. "My car is right here."

I ignored all the warnings about taking lifts from strangers, and gratefully followed the woman into her car. She didn't say anything to me, except to ask where I lived. A couple of times, though, she patted me on the hand, as if to say things were going to be all right.

"Here," I said when we got to our house. What a beautiful house, too. I'd never noticed just how beautiful it was before. The grass was mowed, and there were marigolds blooming in the front garden. Marigolds. If that car had hit me, I might never have seen marigolds again.

"There's no car in the driveway," the woman said. "Are you sure your parents are home?"

"Oh, no, they aren't," I said. "They both work."

"I won't leave you here alone," she said.

"That's okay," I said. "My older sister should be in." I fumbled around, got the key from my pocket, and unlocked the front door. The woman followed me in, to make sure Jean really was there.

She was in the living room, sprawled on the sofa, watching TV and eating an apple. I wanted to hug her.

"You see?" I said instead. "She's here."

"If you want, I'll stay until your parents come," the woman said.

"No, really," I said. "I'm okay."

"Dana?" Jean asked, turning around to face us. "What's the matter? What's going on?"

"You should be very proud of your younger sister," the woman said. "She saved a little boy's life. She's quite a heroine."

And that was the first I realized that I really was one.

2

The next morning at the breakfast table, I was trying to finish my math homework. I hadn't felt like working the night before, and I'd had to tell the story of what happened with the kid to Jean and Mom and Dad so often that I almost believed it had happened. But I didn't think the math teacher would accept it as an excuse for my homework not being done. Jean was nibbling on her toast, and Mom was drinking her orange juice and reading the paper. Dad was upstairs shaving.

"Good grief!" Mom exclaimed, and nearly choked on her juice.

"What?" Jean asked. I didn't even look up.

"There's an article here about Dana," she said.

That was enough to arouse my attention. So I put aside the math, and got up to see what Mom was talking about.

Sure enough, the *Herald* had an article on page 28, all

about what had happened. "Mystery Girl Saves Tot's Life" the headline read.

I tried skimming the article, but it wasn't easy with Mom calling to Dad to come downstairs, and Jean reading it out loud.

"Listen to this," Jean said. " 'I'd know her anywhere. She was about fourteen years old, and she was wearing a red shirt.' Fourteen."

"Do I really look fourteen?" I asked.

"No," Mom said. "The woman was in a state of shock. Bill! Come down here!"

"If Dana looks fourteen, I must look sixteen," Jean said. "That's only fair."

"I wasn't wearing a red shirt," I said. "But it's got to be me."

"Of course it's you," Mom said.

"What's all the excitement?" Dad asked. He still had lather over half his face.

"Look at this," Mom said, and she took the paper away from me before I had a chance to finish it. I didn't think that was fair, since it was about me, but Dad started reading the article before I had a chance to protest. "Would you look at that," he said. "You're famous, Dana."

"She isn't famous yet," Jean said. "Nobody knows Dana's the one who saved that kid."

"Can I tell the lady?" I asked.

"I don't see why not," Mom said. "I'm sure she wants to thank you in person."

"That's what the article says," Jean said. " 'I owe my child's life to this girl. I won't be happy until I can thank her personally.' "

"We wouldn't want her to be unhappy forever," Dad said. "I think Dana should go to the paper after school and let them know. They can contact this woman."

"Why can't I go before school?" I asked. What a great excuse not to finish my math.

"Because school is more important," Mom said. "This can wait. Now, finish your homework, and then you'd better get going."

"Do you think they'll put my picture in the paper?" I asked.

"They might," Dad said. "I guess we'd better prepare ourselves for life with a celebrity."

"All I did was . . ." I started to say. But then I realized what I did was save that kid's life. Who knows? The kid might grow up to be president. Or cure cancer. And it would all be thanks to me. I smiled.

"I think the next few days are going to be absolutely unbearable," Jean said, looking at me. "Anybody mind if I change my name?"

"No teasing," Dad said. "Face it, Jean, you're as proud of Dana as the rest of us."

"I guess," she said, and then she smiled at me. "Sure, why not? My sister, the heroine."

I have to admit I liked the sound of it.

It wasn't easy making it to lunch without telling Sharon the whole story, but every spare minute I had until then I spent on my homework. It was hard concentrating on homework when I knew I was going to go to the paper after school and become famous. The little Dutch boy with his finger in the dike probably didn't have to do his homework for a week after he'd saved Holland. But there were no such breaks for me.

"Did you see that article in the paper?" I asked Sharon as soon as we sat down with our trays.

"What article?" Sharon asked.

"This one," I said, pulling it out of my schoolbag. It hadn't been easy getting Mom and Dad to agree that I should have the one copy of it. But they decided they could buy more on their way to work, so they let me take mine to school.

Sharon skimmed the article. I practically knew it by heart. Another reason my homework hadn't gotten done. "What about it?" she asked.

"That's me," I said. "I'm the fourteen-year-old who saved that kid's life."

"What are you talking about?" she asked, and then she read the article more carefully. "You're not fourteen, Dana. And you were wearing an orange shirt yesterday, not red. How can it be you?"

"It was me," I said, grabbing the article back from her. "It was after we had our ice cream cones. There are witnesses and everything."

Sharon looked at me and laughed. "You're crazy," she said.

"I am not crazy!" I cried. "That's me they're writing about. And Mom and Dad said I could go to the paper after school and let them know it was me. They might even run my picture in the paper."

"Dana, you're my best friend," Sharon said. "I've known you forever. You would never do anything that brave. I'm sorry, but you just wouldn't."

"What are you talking about?" I asked. I was too upset to start eating lunch, even though it was chili, my favorite. Instead, I fingered the article and tried not to pout.

"Dana, you're afraid of your own shadow," Sharon said. "I remember when you wet your pants just because of a little lightning."

"I was in kindergarten then," I said. "And it wasn't just the lightning. I was too scared to ask where the bathroom was."

"See what I mean?" she said. "You were too scared to

ask where a bathroom was, and you expect me to believe you ran in front of a car and saved some kid's life? Really, Dana."

"But I did," I said. "Besides, I wasn't scared to ask about the bathroom. More like shy. Embarrassed. And I really did save the kid's life. I didn't think about it. I just did it. And if that kid cures cancer someday, it's going to be because of me."

"I think you've gone crazy," Sharon said, then started eating her chili. "So did you work on your book report?"

"I didn't work on anything!" I shouted. "Listen to me, Sharon. I'm the person they're looking for. I saved that kid's life. That seemed a little more important than some dumb book report. And I don't understand why you won't believe me. Have I ever lied to you before?"

"No," Sharon said. She stopped eating her chili and looked me over thoughtfully. "You're not a liar."

"Thank you," I said.

"It's just hard to believe, that's all," Sharon said, and went back to her chili.

"I'm going to the paper after school," I said. "I was going to ask you if you wanted to come with me, but since you don't believe me, I guess there isn't any point."

"You're really going?" Sharon asked.

"Of course I am," I said. "I told you my parents said I could."

"That's an awfully long walk for a practical joke," she said.

"Don't come," I said. "Don't see a mother's grateful tears." That had been my favorite phrase in the whole article.

"If I go with you, will you really go through with it?" Sharon asked.

"If it isn't true, I'll treat you to ice cream," I said. "A sundae. Deal?"

"Deal," Sharon said.

I didn't much like the idea that Sharon believed in ice cream more than she believed in me, but I was glad to have company when I went to the paper. I could have asked Jean, but she was fourteen, and looked enough like me that I was afraid the woman might think Jean was the one who saved the kid's life. Sharon doesn't look anything like me.

School that afternoon was even harder to concentrate on than school that morning. I thought I would scream when the clock only moved one second at a time. Fortunately none of my teachers called on me, so I didn't have to let everybody know I didn't have the slightest idea what was going on. If Sharon hadn't believed me, I doubted anybody else would accept my explanation.

When the final bell rang, I jumped up, grabbed my

books and Sharon, and practically pushed her out of the building.

"What's the hurry?" she asked. "You'll be just as much a heroine three minutes from now."

"I want to get it over with," I said. The truth was, the longer the day had gone, the more uncertain I'd gotten. Maybe two kids' lives had been saved the day before. Maybe the lady wouldn't recognize me. The longer I waited, the more her memory would fade. I just wanted to have it done with.

So I forced Sharon to keep pace with me, and I half ran to the paper. I knew where it was, but hadn't been inside it since our class trip in second grade.

"We're going to die of heart attacks before we ever get there," Sharon said, puffing by my side. I'm in better shape than she is.

"It's only four blocks more," I said. "Come on, you can do it."

"I want to live!" she screeched at me, but I ignored her. I had my moment of destiny waiting for me four blocks away. If she couldn't make it, that was her problem.

We were both panting pretty hard by the time we got to the newspaper building. I didn't protest when Sharon raised her hand up to stop me from going in until we both caught our breath. She took out a comb and combed her hair, then offered it to me. I combed mine as well. If they were going to take a picture of me, I wanted to look neat.

"Come on," I said, and walked into the building. I straightened myself as best I could, and tried to look fourteen. But my stomach was hurting and my heart was beating and all of a sudden I started worrying that I'd dreamed the whole thing up.

"Yes?" the receptionist asked.

"I'm the person in the paper," I said. "I mean that article about the mystery girl who saved the tot's life. That's me."

"Oh," the receptionist said, raising her eyebrows. She didn't look like she believed me, and she didn't even know me.

"She really is," Sharon said. "Honest."

I turned around to face her. "Why do you believe me now?" I whispered at her.

"You're not crazy enough to do this if you didn't really do it," she whispered back.

The receptionist looked at both of us, but then she pressed a few buttons and said, "Mrs. Marsh, there's a girl here who claims she's the one who saved that child's life."

I stood there, not even breathing.

"All right," the receptionist said, and hung up. "Girls, Mrs. Marsh would like you to go to the city room and talk with her. She's waiting for you. Straight down the hallway and then it's the first left."

"Okay," I said, and Sharon and I started walking that way. Sure enough, the city room was easy enough to recognize, and Mrs. Marsh was standing there by the door. She'd written the article about me. I'd never met a reporter before, and I felt even more nervous. But Mrs. Marsh didn't look scary. Actually, she sort of looked like my mother.

"Which one of you?" she asked.

"Me," I said. "I mean I. My name is Dana Alison Parker, and I saved that kid's life."

"Come on over here," Mrs. Marsh said, leading Sharon and me to her desk. "Could you tell me a few details about what happened yesterday, Dana? Just to make sure we're talking about the same thing."

"Sure," I said, and I told her the whole story. I'd told it often enough the day before. I made sure to mention the businessman who picked up my books from the street, and the woman who'd been driving the car and had two of her own, and the woman with the Woolworth's bag who'd taken me home. "The kid was wearing overalls," I said. "And a blue shirt, but I didn't know if it was a boy or a girl. It's hard to tell sometimes."

"You certainly sound like you were there," Mrs. Marsh said. "A lot of what you told me wasn't in my article."

"Dana wouldn't lie," Sharon said. "Are you going to call the lady and let her know?"

"Yes, I think I will," Mrs. Marsh said, and sure enough, she dialed a number. Before I knew it, Mrs. Marsh was saying, "Mrs. McKay, I think we've found your heroine. Would you like to come down to the paper and meet her? Fine. We'll expect you here in ten minutes." She hung up the phone and smiled at me. "Can I get you something?" she asked us. "A soft drink, maybe?"

"No, thank you," I said, and Sharon shook her head.

"Wait here," Mrs. Marsh said. "We're going to want some photographs." She got up and went to the other end of the room.

"Do you think there'll be a reward?" Sharon asked me.

"A reward?" I asked.

"Well, you did save that kid's life," she said. "And he might cure cancer, just like you said."

"A reward," I said. What would I do with a reward? And how much might it be?

But I didn't like the way my mind was going. I didn't save that kid's life just to get some money. I didn't even do it to get my name in the paper, or to earn the respect of everybody I knew. I still wasn't sure why I did it, but it wasn't for any sort of profit.

Of course thinking about a reward made the minutes go a lot faster. Mrs. Marsh came back with a photographer, who was holding an awfully big camera with a huge flash attachment. He winked at me, but I started getting nervous again. Mrs. McKay might not recognize me. I couldn't be sure I'd recognize her, and I'd been a lot less upset than she was.

But then Mrs. Marsh started walking toward the door, and I recognized Mrs. McKay all right, and her little boy. Sharon and I both stood up, and I had this horrible thought that Mrs. McKay would walk over to Sharon and thank her by mistake.

But I didn't have to worry. With the photographer clicking and flashing away, Mrs. McKay swooped up her boy and ran to me. "It's her!" she cried as she got closer to me. "Oh, how can I ever thank you?" And soon she was hugging me and the little boy, and the photographer was going crazy, and Mrs. Marsh was taking notes, and Sharon was looking at me almost respectfully. "Oh, thank you, thank you, thank you."

And I swear she cried grateful tears right on me.

3

I liked being a celebrity.

There was an article about me and the McKays on page five in the paper the next day, how Mrs. McKay had found me, and what a heroine I was. I got interviewed and explained how I didn't think, I'd just seen the little boy in trouble and rescued him.

They didn't print that I didn't know if it was a boy or a girl, and they had an awful time getting a good picture of Mrs. McKay, her son Timmy, and me together. Timmy took one look at me and started screaming. I guess he thought of me as the big kid who pushed and grabbed him and scared him a lot more than any car ever had. But the photographer got us posed so Timmy's face was buried in Mrs. McKay's shoulder and you couldn't see that he hated my guts.

"He doesn't really," Mrs. McKay said apologetically. "He's just shy around strangers. And it's so noisy here."

It certainly was noisy, with all those people milling around and talking. The editor of the newspaper even came out and had his picture taken with us.

"I'm very proud that the *Herald* has helped unite this grateful mother and heroic girl," he said, while Mrs. Marsh took notes. "It's just another example of our commitment to this community. But perhaps it's a happier moment than usual."

I wasn't really listening to him, but that's what the article about us said the next day, so I guess that's what he said.

Once Mrs. Marsh had written down everything, and the photographer had snapped enough pictures, and Mrs. McKay and Timmy had left, Sharon and I stood there.

"It's not fair," Sharon said.

"What?" I asked.

"You said if it wasn't true, you'd treat me to ice cream," she said. "Only it was true, and I want ice cream anyway!"

Mrs. Marsh laughed. "I think petty cash can afford to treat you," she said, and she took out her wallet and handed me a five-dollar bill. "Banana splits, courtesy of the *Herald*. Enjoy them, girls."

"I told you there'd be a reward," Sharon whispered as I took the five dollars from Mrs. Marsh.

"Thank you," I said. "You really don't have to."

"Take it, kid," the photographer said. "That's an average day's pay around here."

Some of the reporters laughed. I just smiled, whispered to Sharon that we should go, and reluctantly left. That many adults had never made that much of a fuss over me, except maybe when I was born. I could have stayed there forever, but we had to get our ice cream.

With five dollars, we had plenty of money to treat ourselves to sundaes. I felt a little guilty that we didn't get banana splits, but neither one of us much liked them. So it was hot fudge with mountains of whipped cream instead.

"You should have gotten a bigger reward," Sharon said, wiping the fudge from her lips. "A hundred dollars maybe. Mrs. McKay didn't give you anything."

"She didn't have to," I said. "Be grateful for free sundaes."

"If it hadn't been for me, you wouldn't have even gotten that," she pointed out. "You should let me be your manager."

"I don't think I have much of a career being a heroine," I said.

"You're right about that," Sharon said, and gave her spoon one final lick. "Definitely a one-shot deal."

"What do you mean by that?"

"Oh, come on now, Dana," she said. "Sure, maybe you

accidentally did something brave once, but that doesn't mean you'll ever be brave again."

"What makes you think you would have saved Timmy?" I asked. Now that he had a name, the whole thing seemed a lot more real to me, like it had been my destiny to save Timmy McKay's life.

"I don't know what I would have done," Sharon said. "All I know is you'd never do it again."

"You're just jealous," I muttered, but if she heard me, she didn't pay any attention. Instead, she looked at her watch and told me we should get going. So I paid, and thought about how risking my life had won me an ice cream sundae and twenty minutes worth of attention. I didn't feel so happy anymore.

But that changed when I got home and told Jean, and then Mom and Dad, all about Mrs. McKay and Timmy and everything at the paper. They were proud of me all over again, and promised they'd buy an extra copy of the paper the next day so I could have one for my scrapbook.

We were all surprised the next morning when the picture of me and Mrs. McKay and Timmy with his head turned away from the camera was right on page one, under the headline, where the car-crash picture usually was. "Girl Heroine and Grateful Mother Reunited" the caption read, and then it said, "Thanks to the article in the

Herald, Mrs. Sheila McKay and her young son Timmy were able to thank Dana Parker in person. Dana, aged 13, saved Timmy's life on Monday. Details on page 5."

"Thirteen!" Jean shrieked. "Don't tell me you lied about your age, Dana."

"I did not," I said, wishing the paper had gotten that right. It was a pretty good picture of me, though, and I looked fourteen almost. Definitely thirteen. "It's a natural mistake."

"You're a natural mistake," Jean said, but then she gave me a friendly pat. "Nice picture, kid. What does the article say?"

The article told about the accident and me and the McKays. It got all the details right, except my age. I loved it, and decided to buy at least five copies, in case something happened to the other four.

"I'm so proud of you," Mom said to me. "Now that I see your name in print, I can really imagine what a courageous thing you did."

"I think this calls for a celebration," Dad said. "How about dinner tonight at Mario's?"

Mario's was my favorite restaurant in the world. We never ate there on weekdays. "Can we really?" I asked.

"Absolutely," Dad said. "The four of us. We'll leave the photographers home, though. All right with you, Jean?"

"It sounds great," she said, and smiled at me. "I haven't eaten with a thirteen-year-old heroine in ages."

The day would have been perfect right there, but it got better. At school kids came up to me and congratulated me for having my picture in the paper. And over the loud-speaker, right after we'd said the Pledge, Mrs. Mann, the principal, made an announcement about me.

"I'm sure many of you know that we have a heroine in our midst," she said to every single kid in that school. "Dana Parker, who is in seventh grade, saved the life of a small child on Monday by running into the path of a moving car and carrying the little boy to safety. I know we are all very proud of Dana and congratulate her on her act of heroism."

Then she went on to discuss how the Drama Club meeting had been canceled, but nobody in my homeroom was listening. Instead they were all applauding me. I thought I would burst.

All my teachers congratulated me that day, and I noticed none of them made me answer any questions—except for Mr. Gallo, my math teacher, who doesn't like me. He gave me the hardest problem to solve, but I came up with the right answer.

In English, instead of doing the assigned work, Ms. Margolis got us to talk about heroes and heroines. She told us as long as there had been people telling stories, there had been stories about acts of bravery. And then she asked us to come up with some.

It took a little while, but then we all knew some. Robin Hood and King Arthur and Molly Pitcher and Rosa Parks and lots of others. It seemed absolutely amazing to me that I was one with them. Me and Joan of Arc. Of course Ms. Margolis didn't put it quite that way, but I knew that was how it was. Maybe just for a moment, but I was one of them.

At lunch, kids actually asked me for my autograph. Sharon raised her eyebrows, and I felt pretty dumb, but I signed people's notebooks and paper napkins.

"I told you I should be your manager," Sharon said. "I'd have charged for those autographs."

"Nobody would have asked for one then," I said, but for a dazzling second I thought about it. Once you've signed autographs, anything seems possible.

After school that day I went up to my room and tried to do my homework. But my mind kept wandering, remembering what it had felt like to see Timmy in danger, and how I had just known I had to save him, that if I didn't, nobody else would, and he would die. I couldn't get over it. What courage, and all from me. I hadn't gotten over being scared of lightning until two years ago, and bugs still frightened me. But I had risked my very own life to save the life of a child I didn't even know.

I started giving serious thought to writing my autobiography.

Mario's is an Italian restaurant, and we've eaten there hundreds of times, but I love going there anyway. There are checked tablecloths, and red cloth napkins, and candles burning on each table. It isn't the kind of place you go to just for a pizza, even though their pizzas are the absolute best.

After all these years they know us at Mario's, but when we went there that night, you could just see them stirring.

"It's the Parkers," the hostess whispered to one of the waitresses. "The best table for them, and tell Mario they're here."

"Yes, ma'am," the waitress said, and she showed us to a corner table. It had never occurred to me that Mario's had a best table, but I loved the idea we were going to get to eat at it. It might just have been a Wednesday night, but Mario's was still pretty crowded, so I felt special knowing we were being shown to the best table.

"Remind me to eat with a celebrity more often," Dad said as we sat down.

Then Mario came out. I'd seen him before, and once in a while he'd walk out and go to the tables asking if everything was all right. But tonight he walked very purposefully over to the corner table, the best table, where we'd been seated.

"Mr. Parker," he said formally to Dad. "Mrs. Parker."

"Mario," Dad replied solemnly.

"It is a great honor for Mario's to be feeding the family of such a noble young lady," he said, and for a second I didn't realize he was talking about me. "Tonight, let Mario's treat you all to dinner. Wine, lobster, whatever you desire, it is our pleasure to serve you."

"Dessert too?" I asked, my eyes popping open.

"Dessert too," Mario said, smiling at me. "Soup, antipasto, please order freely and enjoy yourselves. I have many children and grandchildren, and it gladdens my heart to know there are girls like Dana who would risk their lives to save those of children younger and more helpless."

People had the most amazing habit of bursting into speeches when they saw me lately. Still, I wasn't about to complain.

"Thank you, Mario," Mom said. "That's very generous of you."

"It is just a small gesture," he said, and then he bent over, took my hand, and kissed it. "Enjoy your dinners." And he left.

"Lobster," Jean said.

"Jean!" Dad said sharply. "Let's not impose too much."

"No," Mom said. "Mario made us a very gracious offer and he meant it. He wouldn't have offered if he hadn't. Let's not pig out, but if Jean wants lobster, then she should order it. And we'll have wine, as he suggested."

The funny thing was I ended up ordering spaghetti and meat sauce, which was practically the least expensive thing on the menu. But we all got an antipasto and soup, and Mom and Dad had wine and veal, and then we had tortoni for dessert. Being a heroine could prove to be fattening.

"This has been the best day of my life," I announced after we got home. I'd kicked off my shoes and was resting in the living room.

"You know this is the peak," Dad said. "From here it's downhill."

"That's okay," I said. "I don't think I could take too much of it. But it's been terrific for a day."

"I wouldn't mind it happening to me once in a while," Mom said, stretching out on the couch. "Being a heroine sure seems more exciting than being an accountant."

"There are heroic accountants," Dad said, but he didn't sound too convinced.

"I don't even mind the reflected glory," Jean said. "Not if it means lobster for dinner."

Just then the doorbell rang. "Who can that be?" Mom asked.

"Probably Dana's devoted public," Jean said. I tossed a pillow at her, but since nobody else seemed willing to get up, I did. When I opened the door, I saw Mrs. McKay standing there.

"Come on in," I told her, and I brought her into the living room. I introduced her to my parents and Jean, and they all said hello. It felt weird having her in my house meeting my family. She was carrying a shopping bag with her, and I wondered if maybe Timmy would pop out of it. But of course he didn't.

"I don't mean to impose," she said. "And I know it's late. But I just had to do something to show my gratitude to Dana for saving Timmy's life."

"You don't have to do a thing," Mom said. "Believe me, Dana's had more rewards in the past twenty-four hours than she could ever dream of."

"I knew I couldn't just give her money," Mrs. McKay said. "Timmy means so much more than just money. It would . . . sully things if I gave Dana money. But I felt I had to do something."

"You don't have to," I said, partly because I knew my parents wanted me to, and partly because it was true.

"I raise Persian kittens," Mrs. McKay said. She put her

right hand in the shopping bag and pulled out the most adorable long-haired gray kitten I'd ever seen. "He's a purebred," she said. "Really quite valuable, if you decide to sell him. I have his papers if you decide you want to show him. Please let me give him to Dana. It's just a token, I know, but it means so much to me. And I'd love to repay Dana's gift of life with a gift of life of my own."

Another speech. But I didn't mind, this time. "Oh, Mom, please?" I begged. "Daddy? Please?"

Mom and Dad exchanged glances. And then Dad smiled.

"He's lovely," Dad said. "And I know Dana will take good care of him."

"Forever," I whispered, and took the kitten into my hands. Tiny as he was, he curled up on my palm and started purring for all the world to hear.

"I love him," I said, rubbing his soft fur as gently as I could. "I love him, and I'll take care of him forever and ever."

4

"He's the cutest thing you ever saw," I told Sharon the next day in the school yard. "He's just a bundle of gray fur, and he loves me already. He purrs when he sees me."

"I didn't know kittens that young saw," Sharon said.

"Of course they do," I said. "At first I thought I might name him Mario, because Mario treated my whole family to dinner last night. I told you about that, didn't I?"

"Oh, yeah," Sharon said. "You certainly did."

"But Jean didn't think a gray kitten should have an Italian name. She said he didn't look Italian. Jean loves him too, but he definitely prefers me. He slept in my room last night, in my slipper. Can you imagine?"

"So what did you name him?" Sharon asked, looking at her watch.

"Then I thought I'd name him McKay. After all, Mrs. McKay gave him to me. But my parents didn't think that was a great idea. So then I decided to call him McKat. He'll be McKitten while he's still young. Isn't that adorable?"

"Darling," Sharon said. "Can we go in now?"

"I guess so," I said. "The bell'll ring pretty soon."

"Not soon enough for me," she said. I was pretty sure she was kidding. I started following her in, when I heard my name being called. Sharon kept on walking, but I stopped.

"Dana! Wait a second, hold up!" I turned around and saw it was Brian. I looked around nervously to see if Charlie was anywhere near, and then I felt ashamed of myself.

"Hi, Brian," I said, trying to sound friendly. "What's up?"

"I just wanted to tell you that I think it's great the way you saved that little kid," Brian said. His face was flushed from running, and his shirt was half untucked. If I were Charlie, I'd probably pick on him too. Then I felt really ashamed.

"Thanks, Brian," I said.

"You were so brave," he said. He had a fleck of something brown on his left front tooth. I wanted to scrape it off for him. Instead, I rubbed my tongue over my front teeth, in case I had brown flecks too.

"I guess so," I said, feeling really terrible. Brian was

probably a very nice person. I'd never really given him a chance, and here he was telling me how great I was, and all I could think of was what a mess he was. Not to mention worrying about Charlie, like just being seen with Brian was a contagious disease. "I bet you would have done the same thing," I said, not wanting to bet on it at all. "You see a kid in danger, you just automatically risk your own life."

"It takes a special person to do that sort of thing," Brian said. "I don't think I'll ever be that brave."

"I'm sure you will be, someday," I said. "I wasn't always that brave myself."

"Hey, Brian, trying to prove you're human?" Charlie asked, swaggering over to us. "Hi, Dana. Showing off your scars?"

"I don't have any scars, Charlie," I said, wondering if maybe I did and just didn't know about them. I just barely kept my hand from brushing across my cheeks to see if there were any.

"I always thought you had a brain," Charlie said to me. "I guess I was wrong, though."

"Why?" I asked in spite of myself.

"I see you're hanging around with a real jerk like Brian," Charlie said. He slapped Brian on the back, like he might do if he liked Brian, only he did it really hard, knocking Brian's notebook out of his hand. Brian bent down to retrieve it, and I was sure Charlie was going to kick him in the seat of his pants.

"Don't you dare," I said to Charlie. Brian seemed even more helpless than little Timmy McKay.

"Dare do what?" he asked me, looking innocent. But I'd seen the way his eyes had wandered onto Brian's rear end, and I knew I'd stopped him, if just this once. So I decided to press my luck.

"You leave us alone," I told him, as Brian straightened himself out, not knowing what further harm I'd saved him from. He'd tucked his shirt in while he was bent down, and he looked a little better.

"You can't tell me to leave you alone," Charlie declared, looking at me the way he usually looked at Brian. "This is a free country. I can bother anybody I want."

"It isn't that free a country," I said. "It isn't a free school, I mean. I mean you bother me one more minute and I'll tell a teacher."

"You'd rat on me like that?" Charlie asked, looking all innocent.

"Sure I would," I said. "I have rights too."

"You rat on me, you'll pay for it," he said. "And I mean pay hard. You'll wish that stupid car had hit you instead of that little kid."

"It didn't hit that kid," I said. "I saved the kid, dummy."

"Who are you calling dummy?" Charlie asked, and I

knew I'd gone too far. I started resenting Brian a lot then. He was just standing there, doing nothing to protect me. I'd protected him, after all, even if he didn't know it.

"I'm sorry," I said, figuring Charlie was entitled to that much. I wouldn't like it if he called me a dummy, after all. "You're not a dummy, Charlie. Now will you please leave me alone?"

"You hear that?" Charlie said to Brian. "See, you respect me the way Dana does, I'll treat you the same way I treat her. With respect." He gave Brian another heavy back slap and wandered off, probably to break the legs of innocent kittens. I felt sorry for the kittens, but relieved for myself.

"You stood up to him," Brian said to me. His eyes had gotten all big, and he sounded like he'd just seen a miracle. "I can't believe the way you stood up to him."

"I didn't stand up to him very well," I said. "Honest, Brian, I didn't do anything you couldn't do."

"You really think so?" he asked. "You really think I could get Charlie to stop picking on me?"

"I bet you could," I said. "I never used to be very brave myself, but I've become brave lately. I bet you could too."

"And Charlie would stop picking on me?" Brian asked.

"He might," I said. "I bet he would, too." He'd probably just drop dead from the shock, but I didn't see any point telling Brian that.

"Maybe I will stand up to Charlie," Brian said. "Thanks, Dana."

"You're welcome," I said, not quite sure what I was being thanked for. I just hoped Brian didn't stand up to Charlie and get his legs broken for his efforts. But the way I saw it, that was Brian's lookout. I had enough to do saving little kids, and being a role model for everybody else.

I was doodling in study hall, thinking about McKitten, when some kid came in and handed a note to Mr. Lester, our study hall teacher. He read it, and then called out, "Dana Parker."

So I went up to his desk. Everybody stared at me.

"Dana, Mrs. Mann would like to see you immediately," Mr. Lester said. "Leave your books here—it shouldn't take too long."

Ordinarily, getting called into the principal's office would have really panicked me, but I just knew it couldn't be anything bad. So I smiled at Mr. Lester, to show I wasn't scared, and followed the boy back to the main office.

"Come in, Dana," Mrs. Mann said, after I knocked on her door. So I did. I'd only seen Mrs. Mann once, at an assembly for the seventh graders the first day of school. She looked kind of young for a principal, but nice. Besides, I had nothing to worry about.

"Mr. Lester told me to come," I said, because I couldn't figure out what else to say.

"Yes, Dana, I asked him to," Mrs. Mann said. "Dana, do you know who Mr. Rudoph Ogden is?"

"Sure," I said, gasping just a little. Rudoph Odgen was the last of the Ogdens. The Ogdens had just about built our town. I'd graduated from Marguerite Ogden Elementary School, and in three years would be attending Samuel Ogden Senior High School. The library was the Henry and Isabelle Ogden Public Library, and the hospital was Ogden Memorial Hospital, named after all those dead Ogdens who hadn't gotten anything specific named for them.

Only the junior high had escaped being named Ogden, and the rumor was that after Rudoph Ogden died, we'd be renamed for him. In the meantime we were Jefferson Junior High School, which was kind of a nice break.

"I got a phone call this morning from Mr. Ogden," Mrs. Mann said. "He read about you in yesterday's newspaper, and after giving it some thought, he decided he'd like to meet you."

"What was there to think about?" I asked, and then I realized that didn't sound right. "It's no big deal to meet me."

"Mr. Ogden is a very cautious man," Mrs. Mann said. "In any event, he'd like you to visit him today after school, if that would be convenient."

"Today?" I asked. "Why?"

"I don't know for sure," Mrs. Mann said. "But Mr. Ogden takes his civic responsibilities very seriously. And I think he wanted to thank you personally for your act of heroism."

I guess if you have an entire town named after you, you have to take these things seriously. "I can go over there," I said. "Right after school?"

"That's what he said," Mrs. Mann said. "He'll probably serve you tea."

"Okay," I said. I would have preferred another ice cream sundae, but maybe there'd be cookies. I really had to make a record of all the free food I'd gotten out of this. "How do I get there?"

"It isn't too far from here," Mrs. Mann said. "Do you know where the Flowering Grape condominiums are?"

"The new development? Sure." Sharon lived there.

"The Ogden estate is about a quarter of a mile away from there. You just walk past the condos and keep walking," Mrs. Mann said. "It's quite an estate. You can't possibly miss it."

"Okay," I said. "Thank you, Mrs. Mann."

"You're welcome, Dana," Mrs. Mann said. "I know you'll behave in a way to make us all proud of you."

"Yeah," I said. It hadn't occurred to me that I had to

behave any particular way. "Do you think I should bring something?"

"Like what?" Mrs. Mann asked.

"I don't know," I said. "My parents bring wine when they go visiting."

Mrs. Mann laughed. "I don't think that will be necessary," she said. "Just smile and say thank you a lot, and you should do fine."

So I practiced by smiling and thanking her. Visiting Mr. Ogden didn't seem like the best way in the world to spend a sunny afternoon, but I took my civic responsibilities very seriously too.

"I'll walk home with you," I told Sharon after school. "Okay?"

"Sure," she said. "But don't you want to go straight home and play with your kitten?"

"I'd love to," I said. "But Mrs. Mann told me Mr. Ogden wants me to go over to his house."

"Rudolph Ogden?" Sharon asked. "That Mr. Ogden?"

"That one," I said. "And his house is right past yours, so we can walk home together."

"I don't believe it," Sharon said, and we started walking away from the lockers. "Why aren't you excited?"

"What's to be excited about?" I asked. As we walked outside, I saw Charlie picking on Brian again. I guess

Brian just wasn't ready yet to stand up to Charlie. Maybe in another ten or fifteen years.

"Mr. Ogden practically owns this town," Sharon said. "And he's a widower and he doesn't have any kids."

"I know," I said. "He's the last of the Ogdens." I giggled. It sounded like the Last of the Mohicans.

"Honestly, Dana," Sharon said. "Why do you think a man like that would want to waste his time with somebody like you?"

"I don't know," I said. "All I know is Mrs. Mann told me to go over there and behave myself."

"You'd better behave yourself," she said. "Dana, you knucklehead, I bet he's asked you over so he can give you something wonderful."

"I hope it isn't another cat," I said. "My parents were just barely willing to let me have one."

"I don't mean a cat," she said. "I mean something terrific, like a four-year scholarship to the college of your choice."

"Are you crazy?" I asked. "Why should he do that? He doesn't even know me. And college isn't for years yet."

"What else can he do with his money?" Sharon asked. "He's practically ancient. And when he dies, his money is just going to go to charity. So why shouldn't he start giving it away now to worthy kids? Kids like you."

"You really think so?" I asked.

"I'm sure of it," Sharon said. "And I bet Mrs. Mann thinks so too, and that's why she told you to behave yourself. You'd better be just perfect, Dana, or you could be blowing the chance of a lifetime."

"Wow," I said. "If I got a scholarship, then there wouldn't be any problem about Jean and me going to college at the same time."

"Let me check you out," Sharon said, and pulled me over to the edge of the sidewalk. She brushed my hair back, told me to tuck in my blouse, and spit on her hand so she could wipe off some dirt from my cheek. "I guess that'll have to do," she said, but you could tell she was upset that I didn't have my best clothes on.

"I'm clean," I said. "I took a shower last night."

"Now, what are you going to say when you meet him?" Sharon asked.

"I don't know," I said. "How do you do, I guess."

"Okay," she said. "It's better to seem shy than too brash. Remember, do whatever he tells you to do."

"Mrs. Mann said he might serve me tea," I said.

"Drink it," Sharon said. "Whether you like tea or not."

"It's okay," I said. "I'd rather have milk."

"Just don't ask for it," she said. "We don't want him to think you're pushy. Just a polite and very brave person."

"Should I curtsy?" I asked with a grimace.

"Nobody likes a smart aleck," she said. "Promise me you'll behave yourself."

"I promise," I said.

"And I want to hear about everything when you get home," she said. "Promise me you'll call first thing and tell me everything."

"I won't leave anything out," I said. I couldn't figure out why this was so much more interesting than McKitten, but maybe Sharon just needed time to get into things. She never did well on tests during first period.

"Well, I'd better go in now," she said. We'd reached her apartment, and I hadn't even realized it. "You shouldn't be late for your appointment with Mr. Ogden."

"No, I guess not," I said, suddenly very scared.

"Remember to be polite," Sharon said. "And act surprised when he offers you the scholarship. Maybe even say something about having to talk it over with your parents."

"Of course I would," I said. "But okay."

"Call me," she said. "Oh, I wish I could go with you."

"I wish you could too," I said. "Wish me luck."

"You make your own luck," Sharon said. "Good luck, Dana."

I scratched my head trying to figure that one out, but I decided she probably meant if I hadn't saved Timmy

McKay, none of this would have happened. Let alone what was going to happen. I patted my hair back to shape, and walked to Mr. Ogden's house.

It was quite something. The front yard was acres and acres of manicured lawn, with a beautiful garden of mums of every possible mum color. All the trees looked like they'd been planted there with a purpose. And the house was huge and white and had genuine columns. I tried to count the number of windows in the front of the house, but I lost count after ten. Just looking at that house made me think maybe Sharon wasn't crazy.

I rang the doorbell, trying to keep from shaking. A maid opened the door. "Miss Parker?" she asked.

I nodded. Somehow I hadn't counted on a maid. But with all those windows, Mr. Ogden probably had a thousand of them. One for each window at least.

"Mr. Ogden is expecting you," the maid said. "Come this way."

So I followed her through a hallway that seemed to be loaded with Greek statues and paintings that just had to be done by Rembrandt and people like that. We walked past a couple of doorways that I would have loved to look into, and then I was deposited in what I guessed was Mr. Ogden's library. The walls were lined with books, and there was a huge marble fireplace, with a painting over it of one of the Ogdens. I think the senior-high Ogden.

Rudolph Ogden was sitting in a brown leather chair that looked rich and comfortable. He half rose when he saw me, and then gestured that I should sit down on the chair across from his.

I was very happy to sit down and give my knocking knees a break.

"So you're the young lady who saved that child's life," he said to me. His hair was all white, but he didn't look that much older than my grandfather, who retired just last year and still plays tennis every weekend.

"Yes, sir," I said. "I didn't mean to. It just happened."

"You're being very modest," he said, and he smiled at me. It wasn't a kindly-old-man smile. It was more like the smile Dad uses when he has to visit his aunt and uncle, whom he absolutely despises but has to be polite to. "You were very courageous."

"I guess," I said. "I mean, thank you, Mr. Ogden."

"I said to myself, I want to meet this girl," Mr. Ogden continued. "To show her how grateful I am that she would do such a brave thing. I like to think of myself as representative of the citizens of Ogden."

"Yes, sir," I said. He certainly did take his civic responsibility seriously.

"So on behalf of the citizens of Ogden, I'd like to present you with this token of our gratitude," he said, handing me a book.

"Oh," I said. "Thank you." Maybe it was a first edition of something famous.

"It's a history of the Ogden family," Mr. Ogden said. "I wrote it myself, and had a few thousand copies run off, to give to very special people. I hope you'll enjoy it."

"I'm sure I will, sir," I said. "Thank you."

"Very well," he said. "Thank you for coming over, young lady. Enjoy your book."

"I will, sir," I said. "Thanks again." I waited a moment, to see if he was at least going to offer me tea, but he didn't act like he was about to. So I rose, thanked him again, and walked out of the room, taking one last look at it.

I just hoped Sharon would forgive me when I told her that not only hadn't I gotten a four-year scholarship, but Mr. Ogden didn't even remember my name. I knew it wasn't my fault, but you never could tell.

Cookies would have been nice too.

5

"Isn't he the cutest thing you ever saw?" I asked Sharon the next day. We were sitting in my living room, after school, watching McKitten climb up the sofa. He was so tiny he couldn't jump up, but had to claw his way to the top. Whenever it got too hard for him, he stopped for a moment and meowed.

"He is darling," Sharon said, like it hurt her to admit it. She hadn't sounded too cheerful about anything since I called her the night before and told her about Mr. Ogden. I couldn't see why she should be annoyed at me; I would have given me a full scholarship and the keys to the city while I was at it.

"And he's so brave, too," I said, as he finally made it to the sofa. He strolled around on it for a moment, then looked back down at the floor and meowed. "You can do it," I told him, and sure enough, he jumped off all on his own. "See?" I said to Sharon. "A real hero. He definitely takes after me."

"You aren't going to keep that up, are you?" Sharon asked.

"What?" I asked, stroking McKitten. His purr filled the room.

"That business about being a hero," she said. "Nobody cares anymore. If they ever did, which I seriously doubt."

"Care about what?" I asked. "Sharon, what are you talking about?"

"I'm talking about how you've been walking around all week like you're the most important person on earth. One free meal and honestly, you'd think you won the Nobel Prize or something."

"It was more than one free meal," I said. "And I do not act that way. And even if I did, it isn't because Mario himself let my whole family eat there for absolutely free. It's because I saved a child's life. All by myself. With no help from anybody else. And I haven't been acting at all differently. Everybody else has."

"You should hear yourself," Sharon said. "You sound just like you've been behaving all week. You even walk differently."

"I'm walking like a hero," I said. "Tall and proud."

"You're walking like your halo might fall off if you

walked normally," she replied. "And you have this far-away look all the time. Like you're thinking about the movie they're going to make of your life. The teachers have been letting you coast out of charity, but if you don't start paying attention in class real soon, you're going to wish that car had hit you."

"You sound just like Charlie," I shrieked. "I thought you were my friend, Sharon."

"I certainly am your friend," she said. "Nobody else would have put up with you this long."

"It's only been since Monday," I said. "Tuesday really. And today's Friday. That isn't exactly forever."

"That's why I've been sticking up for you," Sharon said. "You should hear what everybody else is saying about you."

"What's everybody else saying?" I asked.

"Oh, you know," she said with a shrug of her shoulders.

"I don't know, Sharon. I don't know anything. Are you going to tell me or are you just going to tease me?"

"Oh, all right," she said. "They've been saying you've gotten really stuck-up. Full of yourself. Just because you got your picture in the paper and Mrs. Mann made an announcement about you."

"I am not acting stuck-up," I said.

"That's not all they're saying," she continued. "They're saying it's all so dumb. Unfair even."

"What's unfair?" I asked. "I did save that little boy's life."

"So you keep saying," Sharon said. "But it's the way you act like doing brave stuff is perfectly normal for you. Like you were Wonder Woman. We all know you, Dana. We all know you're just a little coward who did one brave thing once and will never do another brave thing again."

"I really wish you'd stop saying that," I said. "Maybe I haven't done brave things all my life. But now that I've done one, I'll keep doing them. I've been thinking about becoming a policewoman or a fire fighter or something really dangerous. An astronaut. Because I love taking risks. I love living dangerously. I love saving lives. It's a part of me."

Sharon started laughing. I thought she'd never stop.

"What do you know?" I grumbled. "The bravest thing you ever did was cross the street without holding your mommy's hand."

"I never claimed to be brave," she said. "I certainly never made a big deal out of it, the way some people I know have."

"What do you want me to do?" I asked her. "Save a life a day? It isn't easy. There aren't that many opportunities. Not even for a policewoman."

"First of all, I want you to stop going on and on about how you did it once," Sharon said. "Since you asked. Not just for my sake, but yours too, Dana. If you keep talking about it next week, the kids'll all start making fun of you. They've started to already, but they'll stop if you will."

"I didn't exactly plan to tell everybody about it over and over again," I said. "Okay. Next week I keep my mouth shut. Will that be enough to satisfy you, your majesty?"

"You don't have to be sarcastic," she said. "You're the one who asked for help."

"I never asked for help," I said hotly. "I certainly don't need any help from you."

"In that case I'll leave," she said, and started to get up.

"No, wait a second," I said. "Don't go away mad. Not yet."

She looked at me and giggled. "When do you want me to go away mad?" she asked.

I stared at her like she was crazy, and then I realized what I'd said, and I giggled too. It felt better than hollering. "I guess I have been kind of full of myself," I said. "It's all just been so exciting."

"Sure," Sharon said. "That's what I've been telling everybody."

"But the thing is, doing something that brave has really changed me," I said. "I'm just not the same person I was on Monday."

Sharon inched her way over to McKitten and started stroking him. He rolled over onto his back and purred. "What do you mean?" she asked.

"Mom says people act the way they think they're going to act," I said. "Like if you think you're going to do well on a test, you do."

"Studying helps too," Sharon said.

"Sure," I said. "But you can study and think you'll never do well on a test and flunk it. Just because that's how you think you'll do on the test. See what I mean?"

"I guess," she said.

"I always thought of myself as somebody who was scared," I said. "Scared of spiders and lightning and loud noises."

"And snakes," Sharon said. "And heights."

"And snakes and heights," I said. "Until Monday when I really had something to be scared of, and I wasn't. Maybe I was, but I didn't let it stop me. So now I think of myself as somebody who isn't scared anymore. I'm changed. And that's why it makes me so mad when you keep teasing me about how I used to be. I'm not that scared kid anymore, Sharon, and I really wish you'd stop acting like I was."

Sharon rolled over onto her side, and McKitten rolled over too. She kept petting him and he kept purring. I wished he'd come over to me and let me pet him, but he was having too good a time where he was.

"See?" I asked, not trusting Sharon's silence.

"I see," she said. "I see you're crazy."

"What do you mean by that?" I asked.

"You're still scared of Charlie," she said. "That hasn't changed and it never will."

"I am not," I said. "Not like I used to be."

"It's okay to be scared of Charlie," Sharon said. "That's not my point. All the kids in our class are scared of Charlie. I'm scared of Charlie. He's big and he's mean and you'd have to be crazy not to be scared of him."

"So what does that have to do with me?" I asked.

"If you tell people you're not scared of Charlie, you're lying," Sharon said. "If you really think that one totally out-of-character act has completely changed you, you're lying to yourself. Bravery isn't just doing one brave thing once. It's doing them over and over again, and you'll never do that, Dana. Never."

"Oh yeah?" I said. "Just you watch me, Sharon. I'll show you I'm different. I'll show you how brave I am. Then you'll be sorry."

"Then I'll be shocked," she said, getting up. "I've got to go now. He is a cute kitten, Dana. Have fun with him."

"I'm going to," I said. "He'll always remind me of the person I've become."

"If you say so," she said. "Talk to you over the weekend?"

"Yeah, sure," I said, getting up with her. McKitten looked up, but just rolled over onto his belly.

"Don't be upset," Sharon said. "I know how it is. When my father had his operation, he was just like you. That's all he talked about. We were ready to kill him, but then he started work again, and he stopped talking about his surgery. You should get back to normal next week."

"Good-bye, Sharon," I said, showing her the door.

"Well, you don't have to be so angry," she said. "Good-bye, Dana."

I scowled as she walked down the sidewalk. Part of me really hoped a truck would skid onto the sidewalk and run right into her. Only I'd fly out there and lift her to safety. Then she'd see.

It didn't seem likely, not even to me. I sighed and closed the door.

McKitten was sleeping soundly, and it didn't seem right to disturb him, even if I wanted to play with him. I sighed some more, and then decided to talk to Jean about it. So I walked upstairs to her bedroom and knocked on her door.

"Come in," she said, and I did. She was sprawled on her bed reading a book. Jean reads a lot, and she recommends books she really likes to me. She's really an okay sister, and very understanding at times.

So I told her about what Sharon had said to me. Jean listened thoughtfully and didn't interrupt once.

"You have been kind of unbearable lately," she said when I was finished. "But I figured that would go away with time."

"What do you mean, unbearable?" I asked, close to tears.

"Don't get upset," she said. "We all get like that sometimes. Remember when I won that statewide writing contest?"

I nodded, sniffing deeply. It had been two years ago, and my parents had acted like Jean had written the Great American Novel.

"I was really obnoxious about it," Jean said. "I told everybody. Over and over again, I told them. And I made sure Mom and Dad told every aunt and uncle and cousin, even though I acted like they were just doing it to embarrass me. I even expected people to give me presents just because I'd done well."

"Did you get any?" I asked.

"Dinner at Mario's," she said. "Mario didn't treat, though." She smiled at me, and I felt a little better.

"But you've always been a good writer," I said. "And you'll be a good writer forever and ever. What if Sharon is right? What if that was the only time I'll ever do anything brave?"

"Then you picked an awfully good time to do it," Jean said. "I don't know if I would have saved that kid's life. I might have just stood there, frozen, figuring somebody else would save him. Big Wally and I have talked about that a lot."

"You would have saved him," I said. "I'm not sure Sharon would have, though."

Jean laughed. "I don't know if you've changed," she said. "I do know that for a month or so after I won that award, I was really careful when I wrote a composition. Like it was being judged. And I did better work, and got better grades. I was afraid everybody would think the award was a fluke. And I guess I wanted to prove to myself that I did deserve it. But it wore off after a while."

"I don't want being brave to wear off," I said. "I want to be brave for the rest of my life."

"There's no reason why you shouldn't be, I guess," Jean said. She started fingering her book, so I could tell she was impatient to get back to it. "There's a lot of brave stuff you could do."

"Like what?" I asked.

"You could take a course in lifesaving at the Y," she said. "Then if somebody starts drowning next summer, you could rescue them. Or you could take a course in CPR, and then if you see somebody having a heart attack, you could save them."

"But what if nobody drowns or has a heart attack?" I said. "Then how could I be brave?"

"I can't answer everything for you," she said, which meant the conversation was over. I tiptoed out of the room, since she'd already started reading, and walked back downstairs. McKitten sniffed as he saw me.

"Meow," he said, staring me straight in the eye.

It seemed like as good advice as any.

6

"Hey, Sharon! Wait for me!"

Sharon turned around and stopped. I was glad when she did. It had been a perfectly awful weekend without her. I had thought about calling on Sunday, but I hadn't known if she wanted to talk to me. So instead I had done my homework and played with McKitten and thought about what I could do to prove I really was brave. I hadn't come up with a thing, which left me feeling very discouraged. Sharon might be right after all.

In any event, I made a real point of not opening my mouth all day Monday at school. I wanted to tell everybody about how cute McKitten was, but I was afraid that might lead into explanations of how I'd gotten him, so I didn't. I didn't say anything except when I was called on in class. It was one of the most boring days of my life, but it seemed to work. At least Sharon was willing to wait for me when I called out to her in the school yard.

"Hi," I said, a little breathless from running to catch her. "How are you? How was your weekend? Have you started work on the science project yet?"

Sharon grinned. "Back to normal?" she asked.

I shrugged my shoulders. "I'm trying."

"I had an awful weekend," she said. "I wasn't sure if you were still mad at me, and I didn't know what to do about it."

"Same here," I said, and then I hugged her. "Let's never be mad at each other again, okay?"

"Okay," Sharon said.

"Hey, look at the sweethearts!" Charlie called out from clear across the yard. He'd been standing to the right of the school building tormenting Brian when I'd come out. I hadn't even bothered listening to what he was calling Brian this time. Charlie and Brian had just become part of the school day, like saying the Pledge.

"Ignore him," Sharon whispered to me. "He won't bother us then."

But Charlie brushed Brian aside and charged at us. "Aren't you two pretty," he simpered. "When's the wedding date?"

"Let's just walk away from him," I said, and Sharon and I tried to slip casually out of his reach. But Charlie saw what we were doing and walked faster, so he could catch up with us. I wondered if Brian was grateful to me for saving his neck again. I would have turned around to see, but Charlie was right behind us, and I didn't want him to see me looking.

"Which one of you is going to be the bride?" Charlie called out, and then he laughed. "Or are you both going to be grooms?" He roared at that one, and the other kids in the yard laughed too. I hated all of them.

"I hate him," Sharon muttered, and I could see she was on the point of tears. "Walk faster."

So we walked faster. But Charlie started trotting, and soon he'd caught up with us. "Here comes the grooms," he sang right at us. "I guess you have to marry each other, because no guy would ever want to touch either one of you."

My face was bright red. I yearned for Jean and Big Wally to show up out of nowhere and rescue us.

"It's a good thing you won't be able to have babies," Charlie continued. "The world doesn't need any more ugly people like you."

We were approaching the far sidewalk. I wasn't sure whether Charlie would stop as soon as we were off school property, or whether he'd continue as we walked through town. If he did that, I thought I'd die.

"Here comes the bride. Here comes the groom. The

only way they can do it is with a broom," Charlie chanted at us.

Sharon started crying. Not real hard, but enough so I could see she was. And that made me mad.

"You leave us alone, Charlie!" I shouted. I even turned around too so I could face him. "Go pick on somebody else!"

"Can't you take a little friendly teasing?" he asked. "I thought you were so big and brave."

"Just stop it," I said.

Only he kept coming at us. I knew Sharon would hate it if Charlie saw she was crying. He'd never let her live it down. So I started walking toward him, my fists out. I was just mad enough to hit him, too.

"You touch me, you die," Charlie said, only he sounded cold, like he meant it.

So I stopped absolutely still.

"You want to keep your face, you don't walk one step closer," he said, just loud enough for me to hear him. "I mean it, Dana. Don't come one step closer."

I stood absolutely still. I think I even stopped breathing.

Charlie stood there staring at me. Then he spit at me and turned away, back to the school yard to pick on somebody else.

I didn't know whether to throw up or faint. I didn't do either. Instead I wiped at myself, even though he hadn't hit me, and started breathing again. I was surprised I still remembered how.

"Let's get away from here," Sharon pleaded. I certainly didn't see any reason to stay, so I joined her, and we ran out of the yard. We kept running for a couple of blocks, worried that Charlie might be following us. But he wasn't, so we slowed down after a while.

"That was awful," Sharon said. "I hate him so much."

"You and me both," I said. "I wish I had slugged him."

"You couldn't," Sharon said. "He would have killed you if you'd even tried."

"But I feel like such a failure," I said. "Besides, I read that if you stand up to a bully, he'll just collapse. Like the Cowardly Lion."

"Bullies are only like that in books," Sharon said. "If you'd stood up to Charlie any more back there, you'd need plastic surgery for the rest of your life."

"But if nobody stands up to him, he'll just bully people forever," I said. "He'll turn into a wife beater."

"Then don't marry him," Sharon said. "Really, Dana, you did all you could."

"But I didn't do anything!" I cried. "He spit at me! Do you know how disgusting that is?"

"Yuck," Sharon said. "Did he hit you?"

"No, thank goodness," I said. Just the thought of it made me feel crawly. I shuddered.

"I thought you were pretty brave," Sharon said. "Any braver than that would have been dumb."

"I wasn't brave at all," I said, starting to realize how disappointed in myself I was. "I should have hit him. I should have taken my chances and really hit him. That's what I wanted to do."

"He would have hit you right back, and a lot harder," Sharon said. "How about some ice cream? My treat?"

"Not right now," I said. "Sharon, if I'd been brave the way I thought I was, I wouldn't have let him get away with all that. I would have figured out a way of stopping him. Once and for all."

"Poison, maybe," she said. "You can't outfight Charlie, Dana. It's dumb to even think you can."

"So I'm dumb," I said, and now I felt like crying. All I wanted to be was brave. But now I really worried that everything Sharon had been telling me was true. I was a coward who had just once done something brave. I never would again. All my life I'd wonder what had made me do that one good thing, while I shriveled around in fear. I'd probably get too scared to cross the street or leave the house. I'd turn into one of those people who stay locked up in their bedrooms and only leave their beds to go to the bathroom and eat. Until even the kitchen would get too scary for me, and then I'd die of starvation.

I pictured myself old and withered, down to nothing

but bones and loose flapping flesh. And then I started crying, right in the streets of Ogden.

"Dana," Sharon said. "What is it? What's the matter?"

"I am a coward!" I wailed. "You're absolutely right about me!"

"Oh, Dana," she said, and she put her arm around me. In spite of myself I looked around to see if Charlie could see us. I'd spend the rest of my life looking over my shoulder, watching for Charlie, or the bogeyman, or a bolt of lightning.

"You're not a coward," Sharon said. "Honest. I never said you were a coward."

"You didn't have to," I said. "He spit at me, and all I did was run away. Even Brian stands there and takes it."

"Brian's too scared to run," Sharon said. "Come on, Dana. Stop crying, okay?"

I tried, but I couldn't stop. It felt like I'd wanted to cry for a long time, and there was no stopping it now that I had started.

"What will it take to prove you're not a coward?" Sharon asked. "You want me to get out your press clippings and read to you about how you saved that kid's life? Would that help?"

I shook my head. "I'd never do that again," I said. "It was a fluke. If I'd been thinking at all, I never would have done it."

"How about if I ran into traffic?" she asked. "You think you'd run out and save me?"

"Don't try it," I said. "I can't make any guarantees."

Sharon giggled. That only made me cry harder. I felt like a total idiot, crying in the middle of Main Street, but now that the tears had started, they didn't seem willing to stop. I didn't even have the courage to stand up to my own tears.

"Here," she said, leading me to a bus stop bench. "Sit down and let's think about this."

"There's nothing to think about," I said, but I did feel better once we were sitting. "Everything you said about me was right. I'm just scared all the time. Everything scares me. I never told you this, but I'm even scared of birds."

"Birds?"

"I worry sometimes that one'll swoop down and land on my head," I admitted. "Or peck my eyes out. Not all birds, and not all the time, but sometimes birds really scare me."

Sharon sighed. "Birds," she finally said.

"I know it's dumb," I said. "But birds scare me. Like lightning, and bugs and snakes."

"Do plants scare you?" she asked. "You know, man-eating plants?"

"No," I said. "Plants don't scare me."

"Good," she said. "Because there's a giant man-eating plant climbing up your arm."

I shrieked and started brushing my arms wildly. Sharon laughed so hard I thought she'd be sick.

"Sharon," I screeched, once I stopped waving around. "Sharon, I'll kill you."

"No, I'm sorry, really," she said, between gasps of laughter. After I stopped wanting to beat her, I started laughing too. Man-eating plants indeed.

"I'm sorry, Dana," she said. "But I couldn't stand to see you crying."

Somehow I doubted her motives were all nice ones, but it did feel better to be laughing than crying.

"You know what you need?" she said when we calmed down. "You need a test."

"I have enough of those in school," I said.

"A test of bravery," she said. "Something that you can do that'll prove to you you're not a coward."

"I'll do anything," I said. "Just as long as it doesn't involve Charlie."

Sharon pursed her lips. I watched her thinking, and hoped she was coming up with something that would prove I was brave that wouldn't scare me too much.

"I have it," she said. "Graveyards."

"Graveyards?" I repeated. "I don't want to be buried alive."

"Not that," she said. "Although that would be a good test too."

"Sharon!"

"In books they're always scaring kids by having them stay in graveyards overnight," Sharon said. "I've read about that lots of times."

It sounded vaguely familiar to me too. Like bullies folding if you stood up to them.

"All you have to do is stay in a graveyard overnight," she said. "If you can do that, then you'll know you're brave. Or at least not a coward. No coward would ever stay in a graveyard overnight."

"I can't stay overnight," I said. "What would I tell my parents?"

"Okay, not overnight then," she said. "How about until way after dark? You know, when the owls are flying, just waiting to poke people's eyes out. And the bugs are flying around and the ground is alive with crawling snakes. If you can take all that for even a couple of hours, you'll know you're not a coward."

It sounded just awful. My stomach hurt thinking about it. That convinced me it was the perfect test.

"I could tell Mom and Dad that I'm having supper at your house," I said slowly, "and that your mother'll drive me home."

"And instead you could be in the graveyard," Sharon

said. "You could do it tonight even, and then get all of this over with. Please."

"All those things do scare me," I said. "Snakes and bugs and birds."

"Lightning too," Sharon said. "There might be a storm."

"Tonight," I said. "And then I'll know forever I'm not a coward. A coward would never expose herself to all those bugs and snakes."

"And birds," Sharon said. "And man-eating plants."

"I'll do it," I said. "Tonight."

"Terrific," Sharon said.

"Come with me?"

Sharon smiled. "This is your very own test, Dana," she said. "This one you have to do by yourself."

I wasn't happy about it, but I knew she was right. So I nodded, and then we shook hands. Tonight would prove once and for all whether I was a coward, or whether I was the sort of person who really did do courageous things.

7

The scariest part of it all was how easy it was to lie to my parents. I almost never do, which might have been why they believed me. Or maybe it was because I've had supper at Sharon's lots of times, so there was no reason not to believe me.

I would have liked to have had supper at Sharon's before going to the graveyard, but then her mother would have insisted on driving me home, like I told my parents she would, and I wouldn't have been able to get to the graveyard. So instead I went to the library, and stayed there for a while, and then walked over to the deli and bought a pastrami on rye and a bag of potato chips, and took them with me to the cemetery.

It was almost dark when I got there, but there was still enough light for me to find the Ogden section to stay in. I had a list of things to worry about—bugs and snakes and birds and lightning and ghosts—but somehow I figured if any of those things showed up in the Ogden family section, they'd be higher-class versions. Peacocks rather than starlings, butterflies rather than cockroaches. Besides, the Ogdens seemed more likely to have turned into ghosts than your average citizen. If I had schools and hospitals named after me, I'd probably come around after I was dead to check things out.

So I sat down by Marguerite Ogden's tombstone (she was Charles Ogden's beloved wife, and the beloved mother of Mr. Rudolph Ogden) and thought for a while about being dead. What else is there to think about in a cemetery?

After about ten minutes, I decided I was glad I wasn't dead, and glad nobody I loved was dead. So then I had this great fantasy that Mr. Ogden died and in his will he left me a million dollars because I'd saved Timmy McKay's life, and he'd been so taken with me when he gave me a copy of his dumb book. I kept meaning to read the book, and I was kind of sorry I hadn't. I would have known a lot more about Marguerite Ogden and all the other Ogdens I was keeping company that night if I had. I'd be able to identify their ghosts better.

Anyway, I inherited the million dollars, and I promptly read Mr. Ogden's book, which was the least I could do, and I took the million dollars and spent it. If you're going to have a fantasy about a million dollars, there's no point putting the money in the bank. I bought my parents brand-new cars and took all of us on a trip around the world, and I bought Jean thousands of books, and a horse (I remembered she'd wanted one four years ago, and figured she probably still did, but had given up on ever getting it), and I bought Sharon and her mother a house, because I knew they missed having one, and I got Sharon her very own TV set and stereo, and then I got Jean those things too, and a new wardrobe. I put some money away for a car for Jean too, since even with a horse, I figured she'd want a car too. While I was at it, I got Big Wally a car.

Then I started spending money on me. I got me everything I'd gotten everybody else, and my own phone, and the most wonderful record collection, and my own bathroom, and a video tape recorder and tapes of *E.T.* and *Star Wars.*

I wasn't sure how much more money I'd have left after that, so I figured I'd put whatever was left into some safe sort of stock so there'd be money for Jean and me to go to college. I silently thanked Mr. Ogden, and then I ate my sandwich and the bag of potato chips.

By then it was dark. There was a full moon, so it wasn't nearly as dark as it could have been, but the moon made things a little eerie. It was a perfect night for ghosts, and I was glad it wasn't Halloween. Not that I believed in ghosts, but you never can tell what'll show up on Halloween.

The moon was bright enough so that I could see all the tombstones standing with perfect posture, but I could just barely make out the inscriptions. I walked around a little bit anyway, feeling the marble, and running my hands over the inscriptions like they were braille. The marble was strong and cold, and I couldn't figure out a single letter no matter how hard I tried.

It was a pretty good game, though, and it kept me entertained for maybe twenty minutes. Then I sat down absolutely still and stared at the moon for a while. I thought about how there had actually been people on there, and flags and litter. I wondered if I'd ever walk on the moon, or Mars, or some planet where there were other people. I wondered if I'd ever meet Luke Skywalker and Han Solo. I thought about being a leader, like Princess Leia, and how much courage that took. A lot more than it took to stay in a graveyard, I bet.

So then I tried to scare myself, by thinking about snakes and bugs and birds and ghosts and lightning. Only there obviously wasn't going to be any lightning. It was as clear a night as I could imagine, not a cloud in the sky, and hardly a breeze. Just a bright sharp moon. Besides, I had the feeling if there was lightning, it would be perfectly sensible to be scared of it in a graveyard. The best place to be in a thunderstorm was inside, away from it all.

I gave ghosts a real effort. I thought about dead people, and skeletons, and people whose heads had been chopped off, and things that just floated around and you could stick your hand right through them. I thought about the awful wailing noises ghosts made, and how they haunted the people who murdered them, and the people who didn't avenge their deaths, and how even if they couldn't actually kill a person, they could scare them to death.

Only I don't really believe in ghosts. Jean never lets me believe in stuff like that. Jean doesn't believe in anything she hasn't actually seen, except maybe for oxygen, which she's taking on faith. I could just hear her *humph* that ghosts didn't exist, and anybody who thought they did was dumb or a baby. And I wasn't dumb or a baby, and I tended to agree with her.

I was really sorry I couldn't get worked up about ghosts. If you believe in ghosts, staying in a cemetery after dark must be awfully scary. Just the sort of fear I wanted to conquer. But I just couldn't.

So then I thought about snakes. Snakes did scare me, after all. I stared down at the ground and waited for a snake to show up. I must have sat there staring at the ground for twenty minutes. Occasionally I shifted my weight, but basically I just sat there and stared. And I didn't see a single snake. I thought I saw a couple of worms, but they must have just been twigs. I don't much like worms, but you don't die from them.

So then I looked up for a giant vulture to come and poke my eyes out, but there weren't any vultures, and I got a stiff neck from staring up waiting for them. That only left bugs. There were probably lots of bugs there, but they weren't bothering me. It wasn't like I'd stuck my hand into a hornets' nest. I was just sitting in a graveyard minding my own business, and I figured the bugs were minding their own too. Which was fine by me.

I looked at my watch. It was seven after nine. I decided I'd wait until half past nine and then go home. Nine thirty was certainly after dark, and I was pretty sure it would satisfy Sharon. And if I stayed out much later than that, my parents might wonder and call Sharon, and then we'd both get into trouble.

That left twenty-three minutes for me to entertain my-self. I walked around some more, keeping an eye out for vultures and snakes. I made a solemn vow to read Mr. Ogden's book. Maybe I could do a book report on it. Besides, if he did leave me a million dollars, I'd feel guilty if I hadn't even tried to read it.

Then I sang songs for a while. That was kind of fun, actually, singing at the top of my lungs, knowing nobody was going to hear me. I entertained all the dead people with "The Star-Spangled Banner" and "America the Beautiful" and "Yesterday" and "This Land Is Your Land" and "Take Me Out to the Ball Game." I tried a couple of other songs, but I couldn't remember all the words. And I didn't want to sing anything too cheerful because of where I was, which eliminated a lot of songs I did know. Now that I thought of it, "Take Me Out to the Ball Game" didn't seem so appropriate, but it was too late to undo it.

I'm a terrible singer, so it was a good thing they were all dead already. Jean says my singing could kill anybody, not that she sings any better.

It was nine twenty-four by then, and I would have cheated and gone home, except there were only six minutes left, and I would have only been cheating myself. So I felt the tombstones some more, and then I walked back, trying to get out of the graveyard exactly the same way I got in, and I got a little bit lost, and a little bit panicky. I didn't want to get so lost I couldn't find my way out until dawn. That was more of a test of my bravery than I cared for.

But instead of giving in to the panic, I took a couple of deep breaths and really looked around, using the moonlight to illuminate things. After a couple of minutes I decided to walk a little to the left, and sure enough, after another couple of minutes I found myself back with Marguerite Ogden and the rest of her family.

I said good-bye to them and walked out of the grave-yard. I held off congratulating myself until I was officially out of there, just in case I started getting scared about snakes or bugs, but as soon as my feet hit sidewalk, I really started feeling good. I'd passed the test. I'd gone to a place lots of people were scared of, grown-ups too, and I'd stayed there for three hours, and except for when I'd been lost, I hadn't been scared once. And even then I'd been more scared of my parents than anything else. Ghosts had hardly even occurred to me.

Sharon would have to stop making fun of me. I had changed in a week. I was up to any emergency I could find. Nothing scared me anymore.

I almost wished a mugger would jump out at me, so I could beat him up. But there aren't a lot of muggers in Ogden, and if there were any, they were home watching TV. Which was where I wanted to be.

It's a pretty long walk from the cemetery to my house, and I knew my parents would be angry with me if they knew I was walking it alone at night. But the odds were they wouldn't find out. They didn't come out to say hello to Sharon's mother when she dropped me off in front of the house. And they didn't sit by the window waiting for me to come home either. Dad was probably watching a ball game, and Mom was catching up on paperwork or paying the bills. Jean was on the phone or reading a book or doing her homework. When I got home, I'd have to do mine. Telling Sharon about how brave I'd been would wait until tomorrow at school.

I hadn't thought to buy anything to drink, and I was awfully thirsty. I thought about getting something as I walked home, but I figured it would be better to get back as soon as possible. Besides, there was plenty of stuff to drink at the house. Apple juice sounded really good. Just thinking about it made me walk a little faster.

The shortest way of getting home meant cutting through the school yard at Jefferson. There were streetlights there, so I didn't think it would be too dark or scary. Besides, the moon was so bright it would shine my way through. So I made the left turn to cut through the back of the yard—only before I reached it, I saw something that made me stop.

It took me a moment to figure out just what I was seeing. It was a boy, standing in the shadow of the school building. His back was to me, so I couldn't see who it was, or just what he was doing.

I couldn't decide what a boy was doing in the school yard at that hour. I had a reason to be there, even if it was a weird one, but no one else should be there, let alone right next to the school. I thought about calling out, but then the kid started to move, and I just stood and watched in silence.

He took out a can of spray paint and started painting on the back of the school building. "Jefferson Stinks," he wrote in huge letters. The paint ran a little, but the letters were pretty easy to read. The paint looked dark red, but that was hard to tell with the lighting.

It could only be Charlie, I decided. No one else would be writing things on the school building. Knowing that, I felt really scared, and I even backed off a step or two.

Then I felt dumb and cowardly, and I thought about calling out, so he'd have to stop. But before I could get my mouth to work, he moved a little, and I saw he'd written something before I'd gotten there. "Ogden Stinks" was on the wall already, right next to "Jefferson Stinks."

He stood absolutely still for a moment, and I was afraid he was going to turn around and see me standing there staring at him, but he didn't move. Instead, he lifted up the spray can and added "Too" next to "Jefferson Stinks." Then he laughed a little, which really bothered me. Awful as Charlie was, I never thought he was that crazy. I wanted to run then, because with that can of spray paint in his hands, Charlie was a lot scarier than any ghost, but I didn't dare. Instead, I stood there hardly breathing and watched as he looked at his handiwork.

I thought he was satisfied with what he'd done, but I was wrong. He lifted up the can and started spraying some more. At first I couldn't make out what he'd written, but then he moved back, so he could admire all of it.

"Ogden Stinks. Jefferson Stinks Too. C.E."

I couldn't believe it. Not even Charlie was dumb enough to put his own initials onto graffiti. It wasn't like the work needed his signature. We all would have known he'd done it without his telling us.

But I guess he liked what he'd done, because he put down his paint can and started to clap. And as he turned around I caught a glimpse of his face in the light of the moon.

It wasn't Charlie at all. It was Brian standing there by his handiwork, clapping for all the world to hear. Dumb little cowardly Brian scaring the daylights out of me.

As soon as he started clapping, I made a run for it. As long as he was making noise, he couldn't hear my footsteps. I forgot about shortcuts and ran home, back to where things were normal, as fast as I possibly could.

8

At school the next day the rumors changed every half hour.

The first version was nobody knew who had written the graffiti. Then everybody knew it was Charlie. Charlie had admitted it, one version went. He'd denied it, someone else claimed. Charlie had been suspended, expelled, gotten a week's detention, been found innocent. Everyone had a different story to tell. I think Brian and I were the only kids who kept our mouths shut and just listened.

I don't think Brian noticed me checking him out all the time. I couldn't help it. He seemed back to normal, not like the kid I'd seen laughing the night before. Just quiet, easily picked on, not-very-interesting Brian. Obviously listening, but not saying anything. Not even grinning to himself over what he'd accomplished. I started wondering if maybe he had more than one personality, and some other part of him had been the one I'd seen the night before.

By lunchtime the final version came out. It made sense, so I believed it, even though it came from the kids and none of the teachers would confirm it. Charlie had been accused of the graffiti. He'd denied it, but hadn't been believed. He'd been suspended for the rest of the school week, and would have detention for two weeks after that. The punishment was so severe because he'd been in trouble so much in elementary school. That's why he hadn't been believed. Charlie was a creep, so it stood to reason he'd do something rotten like write on the school building.

I was frantic to talk to Sharon. I hadn't dared to call her when I'd gotten in last night. After all, I was supposed to have just left her house; it would have seemed a little fishy if I'd immediately run to the phone to call her. And that morning at school, she'd had the nerve to be late. Her mother overslept maybe once a month, and this had to be that one time. So I was relieved when I could finally get her attention, and talk things over with her in the cafeteria.

Except as soon as we sat down at the table, I saw Brian, sitting all alone in a corner. As much as I wanted to talk to Sharon, I just had to talk to Brian first. I needed to know what to do, and maybe he could be the one to tell me.

Brian might have been feeling lonely, but he wasn't being bothered by Charlie, and he seemed to be enjoying that. At least he had a half smile on his face as he chewed on his tuna salad sandwich. He was the last person in that room I would have picked as a villain.

"Mind if I join you?" I asked, not waiting for Brian to object. I sat down in one of the three empty seats that surrounded him.

Brian didn't seem to mind at all. "Hi, Dana," he said, his half smile turning into a whole one. "Isn't it a great day?"

"You mean because of Charlie?" I asked.

"Charlie's an idiot," Brian said, taking a big bite from his sandwich. "He doesn't bother me."

That made me mad. "I think he bothers you a lot," I said. "And I think you got even with him by writing that stuff last night and signing his initials."

"You're crazy," Brian said flatly. "Is that all you want to talk to me about, Dana?"

"Brian, I saw you," I said. "I saw you do it. It was around a quarter to ten last night, and you laughed before you signed Charlie's initials. You applauded, too, when you were finished, Brian. I saw it all."

He stared at me, and I could tell he was upset. "You didn't say anything," he said.

"You scared me," I said. "I left when you were clapping, so you wouldn't hear me."

"I scared you?" Brian said, and then he laughed. "Boy, that's really funny."

"What's funny about it?" I asked. "I don't scare you, do I?" I sort of hoped I did.

"No, of course not," Brian said. "But I figured you were the bravest person in this school. In the whole dumb town, probably. And you were my inspiration."

"I was your what?"

"I don't usually do stuff like I did last night," Brian said, sounding proud of himself. "But I'm really sick of the way Charlie's been treating me. And I thought about what you would do, how you'd handle it, and I decided to act the way you would. Bravely."

"There's nothing brave about sneaking around in the middle of the night and painting on the school," I said.

"Sure there is," Brian said. "I could have been caught, and then I'd have gotten in real trouble. Especially if I was signing Charlie's initials. I almost wrote his whole name, but I decided that was too obvious, even for him. Don't you agree?"

"That has nothing to do with anything," I said. "Brian, listen to me. I was there. I saw. You did get caught."

"What were you doing there, anyway?" Brian asked. "I didn't think you lived near the school."

"I was out for a walk," I said defensively.

"Your parents let you go out for walks that late?" Brian asked.

"They thought I was with Sharon," I said.

"You mean you were sneaking around too?" Brian asked. "I guess we're more alike than I thought."

"We're not at all alike," I said, but I was blushing. I just hoped Brian didn't notice. "Anyway, that's beside the point. You've got to tell Mrs. Mann you're the one who did it."

"No I don't," Brian said, and started chewing on his sandwich again.

"Of course you do," I said, wanting to ram that sandwich down his throat. "You can't let Charlie get punished for something you did."

"Charlie deserves to be punished," Brian said. "Maybe not exactly for this, but for lots of other stuff. Everybody's really happy he's been suspended, or haven't you noticed?"

"I've noticed," I said. "But that still doesn't mean you can get away with it."

"Who else is going to tell Mrs. Mann?" Brian asked. "Who else knows?"

"I know," I said. "I'll tell." I couldn't believe how dumb Brian was being.

"You tell Mrs. Mann, I'll tell your parents you were out

in the middle of the night sneaking around and lying to them," he said. "Tit for tat."

"That's blackmail," I said.

"Blackmail is when you ask for money," he said. "I don't expect you to pay me for keeping my mouth shut. I just expect you to keep yours shut too."

My mouth went wide open, but no words came out.

"Look at it this way," Brian said patiently. "You tell Mrs. Mann, you get in trouble, I get in trouble, and Charlie comes back and bothers everybody. No one is happy, except maybe Charlie. You keep quiet and the only one who's unhappy is Charlie. And even you have to agree he deserves to be unhappy."

"I . . ." I said but there was nothing to follow that "I." So I started another sentence with "You," but I didn't have anything to finish that one with either.

Brian took one last mouthful of tuna sandwich and then smiled at me. "Think about it, Dana," he said as he got up from the table. "I think you'll know what the smart thing to do is."

I watched as he walked off. Just talking to him had made me feel dirty. If I could have taken a bath then and there, I would have. Instead, I got up, surprised by how shaky I was, and walked back to Sharon.

"That sure was fun," she said, pushing my tray toward

my seat. "First you tell me you have to talk to me, and then as soon as we sit down you disappear."

"I had my reasons," I said.

"I'll just bet," she said. "I think those ghosts got to you. What's the matter? Couldn't you stick it out?"

"Of course I did," I said. "I stayed until way after nine."

"Pretty good," she said. "Now do you think you're officially brave?"

"Charlie didn't paint on the wall," I said. "Brian did. I saw him last night on my way home."

Sharon put her fork down with a loud bang. "You're kidding," she said. "Is that what you were talking to Brian about?"

I nodded.

"Brian?" Sharon repeated. "Dinky little Brian did that?"

I nodded some more.

"Son of a gun," Sharon said. "Who would have thought it?"

"What should I do?" I asked, hoping Sharon would give me a perfect answer.

"What do you mean, what should you do?" she replied. "You keep your mouth shut, that's what you do."

"But that's not fair," I said. "Why should Charlie get punished for something Brian did?"

"Because Charlie is a creep and a bully and he has it coming to him," Sharon said. "If he's going to pick on kids all the time, he has to expect them to do stuff to him too."

"But it's so sneaky," I said. "Sneaky and underhanded, just like Brian."

"I think it's smart," Sharon said. "I wish I'd thought of it."

"You might not like Brian when you hear this," I said. "He's blackmailing me."

"What?" Sharon asked, and then she giggled. I could have killed her.

"He's threatening to tell my parents I wasn't with you when I saw him last night if I tell Mrs. Mann. I'd call that blackmail, wouldn't you?"

"You mean if you rat on him, you'll get in trouble with your folks?" Sharon asked.

"You got it," I said. "I don't know what kind of trouble, though."

"I can imagine lots of stuff," she said. "No weekend privileges or grounding you for a month or maybe even worse."

"What could be worse than that?" I asked, not really wanting to hear.

"They could really punish you," she said. "If they find out I was involved, they could say we can't be friends anymore."

"They wouldn't do that," I said.

"You never know what parents are going to do," Sharon said. "They could make you sell McKitten, and then could keep the money for themselves."

"Sell McKitten?" I asked.

"Or give him back to Mrs. McKay. That's what my mother would do."

I edged my tray of food away. The way I felt, I was never going to eat again.

"All that'll happen if you tell is complete disaster," Sharon said, looking very serious. "You'll get in trouble with your parents, that's guaranteed. Jean won't like it, because it's bound to come out that you're the one who told, and then everybody'll make a fuss and they'll all know she's your sister and she'll have to go around defending you. I won't like it for the same reasons. And everybody'll assume that you saved Charlie's neck just so he won't bother you anymore."

"What?" I asked, my voice squeaking.

"Everyone knows Charlie's been picking on you lately," Sharon said. "They all saw us in the school yard yesterday. If you turn in Brian, and Charlie comes back, people will think you did it to stop Charlie from bothering you. Or even worse, that you like Charlie."

"Nobody'll believe that," I said.

"You never know what people will believe," Sharon said. "That's what my mother always says."

Sharon's mother had been through two divorces and knew a great deal about life. "But that's so unfair," I said. "It's all so unfair."

"Lots of things in life are unfair," Sharon said. "It was unfair of my parents to get divorced. It's unfair that rich people don't pay as much income tax as normal people. It was unfair that Mr. Ogden didn't give you a scholarship. Life's unfair, Dana. You're old enough to know that."

"But why should I be hurt because of something Brian did to Charlie?" I asked.

"Don't you see, Dana, you don't have to be hurt," Sharon said. "All you have to do is keep your mouth shut and everything will be fine. Brian's given you a reason not to tell Mrs. Mann. You shouldn't have to be punished just so Charlie can come back to school. Charlie probably likes being suspended. He does terribly in school anyway. Just don't say anything to Mrs. Mann and everybody will be happy. McKitten can grow up to be McKat and your parents never have to know."

"I have to think about it," I said. It wasn't that I didn't like Sharon's answer to my problem. It was just she'd given me a headache.

"Don't think too hard," she said. "That's when people get in trouble, when they think too hard about something that's really obvious." She smiled at me, but I didn't even try to smile back. There was nothing in my life to smile about that day.

9

The awful thing was I knew Sharon was right. What made it even worse, though, was I knew she was wrong, too. I didn't know anybody could be right and wrong at the same time. Of all the things that were unfair, that seemed the unfairest of all.

Jean was on the phone with Big Wally when I got home. She'd just seen him in school, but that wasn't stopping her from giggling into his ear. I stayed in the living room until I heard her hang up, and then I went into the kitchen. McKitten was curled up on her lap purring. I wanted to grab him from her. If I only had a little more time with McKitten, I wanted him on my lap.

"Hi, Dana," Jean said as soon as she saw me. "I heard what happened to your friend Charlie today."

"He's no friend of mine," I said angrily. McKitten looked up at me but made no effort to move.

"Okay," Jean said. "You don't have to bite my head off. I was just kidding. I bet you're glad he was suspended. As far as I can figure out, everybody in the junior high is, even the ninth graders."

"Even them?" I asked.

"Charlie's the kind of person you have to notice," Jean said. "Even Big Wally doesn't like him."

"But he isn't scared of Charlie, is he?" I asked.

"Big Wally isn't scared of anybody," Jean said. She and McKitten stretched at the same time. "Except maybe his algebra teacher. Here, you want the kitten?"

"Yeah," I said, and, reaching out, took him from Jean. "You like algebra, don't you?"

"It's okay," Jean said. "I promised Big Wally I'd tutor him in it."

"And you like junior high, too, don't you?"

"It's all right," Jean said.

"Even with me there?" I asked.

"To tell you the truth, I hardly even know you are," Jean said. "I've been meaning to thank you for that. I thought you'd be an awful pest the way you were in kindergarten."

"Jean!" I said sharply, and McKitten jumped off my lap at the noise. "I'm not five years old anymore."

"I know," Jean said. "I was wrong, and I'm sorry. You've been sticking with your friends, and you haven't been bothering mine, and I appreciate it. I haven't even minded that fuss they've been making about you in school."

"Well, that was last week," I said. "This week nobody's been fussing."

Jean smiled. "Keep it that way," she said, "and we'll both be happy."

This was not at all what I wanted to hear. If I got Charlie out of trouble, Brian would tell everybody and I'd be center of attention all over again. My stomach really started to ache, and looking at McKitten didn't make things any better. I could live with Jean hating me for a day or two. But if I lost McKitten I'd be miserable for the rest of my life.

"What's the worst thing you ever did?" I asked Jean.

Jean walked over to the refrigerator and poured herself a glass of milk. "What do you mean worst?" she asked.

"The worst thing you ever did that Mom and Dad found out about," I said. "You know, like you lied to them and they found out. Something like that."

Jean concentrated for a moment. "When I was real little, I threw out this teddy bear you'd gotten for your birthday," she said. "You were three and I was five, and I wanted the teddy bear and you said I could have it, only Mom said you didn't understand what I meant and I couldn't keep it. So I threw the teddy bear out. If I couldn't have it, you couldn't have it. That was pretty rotten of me, and I've been sorry ever since." She took a gulp of milk and didn't look very sorry at all.

"What did Mom and Dad do to you?" I asked.

"I can't remember," she said. "I was only five, after all."

"How about something bad you did when you were twelve?" I asked.

"Why?" Jean replied, wiping some milk off her lips. "Are you planning to do something bad?"

"It's none of your business," I said, and stormed upstairs. Teddy bears. When you needed some real advice from a big sister, all you got were stories about teddy bears.

I hardly ate a bite of supper that night, and I certainly didn't hold up my end of the conversation. Instead I stared at Jean and McKitten and Mom and Dad and imagined all sorts of terrible things. I didn't pay much attention when we watched TV that night, even though two of my favorite programs were on. And I went to bed early, hoping that if I fell asleep, when I woke up all my problems would be gone.

McKitten clawed his way up to my pillow and curled up next to my head. It always made me uncomfortable when he did that, so I moved him down to my feet. That excited him and he chased his tail for a while. I could half see him by the light from the hallway. It was hard to imagine anything cuter than McKitten. I wondered what he'd be like when he was a cat, and whether I'd have him long enough to see him grow up.

It took me forever to fall asleep, and when I did I was sorry. I had awful dreams. In one of them McKitten got run over and died, and in another one Mrs. McKay came back and took McKitten away from me, saying I wasn't worthy of him. And then, in the worst dream of all, I was the one painting on the wall and my parents saw me and punished me by throwing me out of the house and the only person who was nice to me was Charlie.

After that I didn't fall asleep even though it wasn't even five yet. Instead I lay on my bed and watched McKitten play. This might be my last shot, and I figured I'd better see as much as I could, so I'd have something to remember him by.

The worst thing about waking up before five in the morning is it gives you a lot of time to think. At first all I thought about was how much I would miss McKitten if my parents really did make me give him up. I thought about how unfair that was. But then I started thinking about how unfair it was that Charlie was being suspended for something he hadn't even done. Who knew what his parents were doing to him when this one time he actually

was innocent? If my parents made me give up McKitten, at least they'd be punishing me for something I was guilty of.

And then I realized how mad I was at Brian for blackmailing me. If I let him get away with framing Charlie and I let him get away with blackmailing me, I might be starting him on a life of crime. He had practically told me I had already. He could turn into something even worse than Charlie, and it would all be thanks to me.

Once I knew all that, I knew I'd have to tell my parents the truth, no matter what it cost me. And just as I decided that, the sun started coming up and McKitten fell asleep and I knew no matter how mad my parents got, they weren't going to take him away from me. I'd be punished, but I wouldn't be hurt. They loved me and they loved McKitten too, and things were going to be okay with them.

As soon as I'd decided what to do, I practically went crazy waiting for everybody to get up so I could make my confession. It was real easy to be brave lying in bed deciding what to do. I wasn't so sure I'd stay that brave when the moment really came.

Mornings can be crazy at our house, with all of us rushing around to get ready to leave. I did what I could, by using the bathroom and getting dressed before everybody else. I even went downstairs and started breakfast, so things would be ready when everybody came down. It helped, too. Before I knew it, or really even wanted it, Mom and Dad and Jean and I were sitting around the kitchen table eating toast and drinking orange juice.

"I have something to tell you," I announced, trying to keep my voice from shaking.

"We figured," Mom said. "What is it, honey?"

"I lied to you about something," I said. "It's a long story."

"We have time," Dad said. "Start at the beginning."

So as we sat in the kitchen with the sunlight pouring in, I told Mom, Dad, and Jean the whole story, from what Sharon had said to me the Friday before through Brian's blackmail threat. It was amazing how much better I felt telling the truth.

"I don't like the idea that you lied to us," Mom said when I'd finished. "I thought you knew better."

"I do," I said. "But if I'd told you the truth, you'd never have let me go. And it wasn't like I was doing anything bad."

"It might have been dangerous," Dad said. "Of course, not many people get mugged in graveyards this time of year. . . ." I could see he wanted to laugh. That was definitely a good sign.

"Stop snickering," Mom said, but then she giggled. "A

graveyard," she said. "I didn't know kids even knew about graveyards anymore."

"It was Sharon's idea," I said. "She thought it would be scary. But I wasn't scared. Telling you the truth is scarier than anything in that graveyard."

"We are going to have to punish you, though," Mom said. "For lying. Because if you lie about something harmless now, you might lie about something a lot more serious some other time. It's a habit I don't want you to get into."

"I know," I said. "I'm sorry. It was dumb of me to do."

"No weekend privileges?" Mom half asked, and Dad nodded. "Just for this weekend, because after all, you did admit what you'd done. But you'll have to stay home this weekend, and no visits from Sharon or anybody else. And no staying up after ten. Fair enough?"

"Fair enough," I said. I didn't know where I'd gotten the idea that they'd take McKitten from me. It was all Brian's fault, and Charlie's, and Sharon's. They were making me as crazy as they were.

"Good," Dad said. "Then that's settled."

"I guess," I said. "But I'm still not sure what to do about Charlie."

"I think you are," Dad said. "I don't think you would have told us everything if you were going to let Brian get away with what he did."

"But I don't know what's going to happen if I tell Mrs. Mann the truth," I said. "Sharon said terrible things would."

"If you hadn't told Brian you knew, nobody would have to know you ratted on him," Jean said. "That was real dumb of you, Dana."

"It seemed like the right thing to do," I said.

"And telling Mrs. Mann is also the right thing," Mom said. "For Charlie and for Brian and for you. This isn't your secret to have to keep, Dana. You feel better for having told us. You'll feel better for telling Mrs. Mann."

I was pretty sure she was wrong. Adults can be sometimes. "Can either of you go with me?" I asked, hoping they'd offer to go without me. Brian might be scared of me if I brought in my parents.

"I don't think we should," Dad said. "I think you've been handling the situation fine up till now and you should keep on handling it."

"Jean?" I asked feebly.

"Are you out of your mind?" she asked. "I don't even want to know you in school anymore."

"Jean!" Mom said sharply.

"No, that's okay," I said. I couldn't blame Jean at all. To tell the truth, I didn't want to know me right then either.

10

I got to school ten minutes early and went right to Mrs. Mann's office. Now that I knew what I was going to do, I couldn't bear the thought of postponing it. I just wanted it all to be over with.

I knocked on her office door and told her who I was, and she told me to come in. I sat down in the same seat I'd sat in the week before when she told me about Mr. Ogden.

"What do you want, Dana?" Mrs. Mann asked. She didn't sound mean or impatient, just curious.

"You know that graffiti on the school wall?" I asked.

"Oh," Mrs. Mann said, "you might say I know it."

"Well, Charlie Everest didn't do it," I said.

"How do you know that?" she asked. "Did he tell you?"

"Oh no," I said. "I hate Charlie. I'd never talk to him about anything."

"Did somebody else tell you, then?" she asked.

"I saw the kid who did it," I said. "I saw him do it, I mean. And it wasn't Charlie. So I really think you should tell Charlie he can come back to school. Because it's unfair he's being punished, since he didn't do it."

"If Charlie didn't do it, who did?" Mrs. Mann asked.

The only way I'd gotten myself into her office that morning had been by convincing myself she wouldn't ask that. I wasn't crazy about the idea of having Charlie like me. But I also knew I didn't want Brian mad at me. I'd seen what Brian could do when he was mad. "Do I have to tell you?" I asked.

"I'm afraid so, Dana," Mrs. Mann said. "Why? Did one of your friends do it? Is that how you saw him?"

"Oh, no," I said. "I wasn't there because I knew anything about it. I was walking home from the cemetery—"

"What were you doing at the cemetery?" she asked.

"That's kind of a long story," I said. "It's personal, but I went to see the Ogden family graves."

"Oh," Mrs. Mann said. "Because you visited with Mr. Ogden?"

"Yeah," I said. This just wasn't the place to go into the whole story. "Anyway, I was going to cut across the school yard, because that's the shortest way back to my house, and that's how I saw it."

"And who was it?" Mrs. Mann asked. "Who did you see painting on the school wall?"

"I still don't understand why I have to tell," I said. "Can't you just tell Charlie to come back?"

"No I can't," Mrs. Mann said. "For a couple of reasons. First of all, I want to punish whoever is responsible. I think you agree that he should be punished, don't you?"

"I guess," I said. I wished I'd never gone there.

"And maybe they did it together," Mrs. Mann said. "Maybe it was Charlie's idea, and that's why his initials were on it. I have to find out."

"Oh, no," I said. "No, there's no way they did it together. They don't like each other at all. It was a frame-up."

"I see," Mrs. Mann said. "Are you ready now to tell me who you saw?"

"Brian O'Shea," I muttered. "That's who I saw."

"Brian O'Shea," Mrs. Mann said. "I don't think I know him."

"He's new," I said. "And he's never been in trouble, and Charlie's been just awful to him. Charlie picks on him all the time, and he makes Brian miserable. Charlie's a horrible person. Everybody hates him."

"But he didn't paint on the walls," Mrs. Mann said. "You're sure of this, Dana?"

"Positive," I said.

"Well, that explains one thing," Mrs. Mann said. "I couldn't understand why Charlie Everest would say things stink. I would have thought he'd use stronger language, but I told myself to be grateful for small favors. And you think Brian signed Charlie's initials to get even with him."

"I think so, yeah," I said. "Can I go now?"

"Yes, you'd better," Mrs. Mann said. "You'll be late for homeroom otherwise. And Dana, thank you. I know it wasn't easy for you to come in here, but you did the right thing. Not even Charlie Everest should be punished for something he didn't do."

"I guess," I said. "You're going to talk to Brian?"

"This morning," she said. "I won't tell him you told me, Dana. You don't have to worry about that."

"He'll know anyway," I said miserably. "But thanks."

"Thank you," she said. "And someday you must tell me why you were in the graveyard. That sounds like a really interesting story."

"Sure," I said. "Someday." I walked out of her office, and cursed my life a few times. I didn't feel any better when I saw Brian get called to Mrs. Mann's office. He gave me a look, and then gathered his books and went off with the messenger. I just hoped he wouldn't kill me when he got back.

I kept waiting all morning for Brian to return to class and get it over with, but he didn't show. I knew none of it was my fault, but I also knew Brian didn't see it that way. I didn't pay attention to any of my classes, and twice my teachers scolded me. The week before when I hadn't paid any attention, nobody minded. I missed those days.

"I've got to talk to you," I whispered urgently to Sharon at the start of lunch. Instead of joining the other kids, we went off to a fairly deserted corner and sat down with our trays.

"I saw Brian get called down to Mrs. Mann's office," Sharon said before taking a bite of her hamburger. "How do you think she found out?"

"How do you think?" I asked. I'd gotten the pizza, and it looked even worse than usual. I used to like lunchtime, too.

"You didn't tell her?" Sharon asked. "What about the blackmail?"

"I admitted everything to my parents this morning. They're punishing me, but nothing too bad."

"You get to keep McKitten?" Sharon asked. I thought she looked a little disappointed.

"Of course I do," I said. "No weekend privileges. And just for this weekend. My parents were very impressed that I told them the truth. After I'd lied to them, I mean."

"You sure got off easy," Sharon said, nibbling on a

french fry. "My mother would have been a lot rougher on me."

"Maybe," I said, taking a bite of the pizza.

"Did you tell your folks I was involved?" Sharon asked.

"Yeah," I said. "I told them everything."

"Great," Sharon said. "Real smart, Dana. What if your parents tell my mother? I could get in real trouble."

"They're not going to do that," I said. "Honestly, Sharon, you're not the one in trouble here. You don't have to dramatize things."

"You're right," Sharon said. "You're in enough trouble for the two of us. Wait until everybody finds out you're responsible for Charlie coming back."

"How is everybody going to find out?" I asked. "I'm sure not going to tell them."

"They'll find out," Sharon said. "You know and I know and Brian must know too. When three people know a secret, it isn't a secret anymore. That's what my mother always says."

"So they find out," I said. "So what?"

"So everybody hates you, that's all," Sharon said.

The pizza lost all its appeal then. Sharon had a point. Nobody liked Charlie, and nobody had anything much against Brian, except maybe me. If I had to pick sides, I sure picked the unpopular one.

"I did the right thing," I said, my voice faltering.

"What does that have to do with anything?" Sharon asked. "But I guess you won't have to worry."

"I won't?" I squeaked.

"Not when Charlie finds out you rescued him," Sharon said. "He'll protect you from everybody."

"I don't want Charlie to protect me," I said. "I still hate Charlie, the same as everybody else."

"You really are crazy," Sharon said. "Having Charlie protect you is your only chance."

"Then I don't want a chance," I said. "Charlie isn't going to find out I rescued him from me."

"Then he'll just go right back to picking on you," Sharon said. "On me, too. Is that fair, Dana?"

"None of this is fair," I said. "Aren't you smart enough to realize that?"

"I can't believe you're calling me dumb," Sharon said.

"I never said you were dumb."

"Well, you certainly implied it," Sharon said, slamming her hamburger down on the plate. All the ketchup squished out.

"I didn't mean to," I said, even though I probably did.

"You do lots of stuff you don't mean," Sharon said. "And all it does is get people in trouble."

"You're a great friend, you know that?" I said. "I come to you with my problems and all you tell me is I'm doing everything wrong. You never back me up. No. It's just

'You're crazy, Dana' or 'You're out of your mind, Dana' or 'You never do things right, Dana.' "

"I'm just telling you the way I see things," Sharon said. "I'd think you'd like an honest friend."

"I can believe the honest part," I said. "But sometimes I wonder what sort of friend you really are."

"I'm not the sort of friend who tells on people," Sharon said. "Unlike some people I could name."

"Oh, shut up already," I said. "I can't do anything right, can I?"

"If you listened to me once in a while, you might," Sharon said. "But whenever you pretend to ask me for advice, you go out and do just the opposite."

"Maybe that's because you give me crappy advice," I said. "You ever think of that possibility?"

"I give great advice," Sharon said. "If you'd listened to me, none of us would be in trouble. Instead we all are. Don't call me dumb, Dana Parker."

"I'm not going to call you anything," I said. "Not ever again. I don't need a friend who treats me the way you do. As far as I'm concerned, we aren't friends anymore. If we ever really were."

"That's fine by me," Sharon said, and took a huge bite out of her hamburger. "Good-bye, Dana," she said, her mouth full of meat. "See you around."

"Not if I'm lucky," I said, and grabbed my tray and my books. I sure wasn't going to keep on eating lunch with Sharon.

But wherever I looked around in the cafeteria, I saw kids all laughing and talking, and not needing me. And I didn't really want to explain to kids I knew why I was no longer eating with Sharon. One explanation would lead to another, and then I'd probably end up with no friends at all.

So I looked around for Jean's table. Ordinarily I would never have eaten with Jean and her friends, but these were desperate times. I made my way across the cafeteria, trying to balance my books and my tray and not show everybody, especially Sharon, how shaky I felt. I just concentrated on looking at Big Wally sitting at the corner table. Jean would be there with him, and she'd take care of me. She had to. That was why you had big sisters, after all, to take care of you.

But when I got to Big Wally's table, there was no Jean to be seen. I tried not to look too crazy as I checked out all her friends to see if one of them was hiding Jean.

"Hi, Dana," Big Wally said. The other kids kept ignoring me.

"Where is she?" I finally asked. "I mean, where's Jean?"

"She skipped lunch today," Big Wally replied. "She said

she wasn't hungry, so she went to the library. Why, Dana? Is something going on?"

"Oh, no, nothing," I said, and before I knew it I was giggling so hard I didn't think I'd ever be able to stop. I knew it was better to giggle than to cry, but not by much. Not by very much at all.

11

I wasn't really counting on a snowy day at the end of September, but a hurricane would have been nice. Instead, the next day was bright blue and sunny. Just my luck.

Of all the places I wanted to be, school was last on the list. An emergency dentist's appointment would have seemed like heaven just then. It wasn't like I knew just what was going to happen in school that day, but I dreaded whatever it would be. Charlie was bound to be back, Sharon was no longer speaking to me, and Jean was acting like I had the plague. The only thing I really had to look forward to was Brian being suspended. At least I wouldn't have to deal with him.

But that wasn't enough to make me want to go to school. "I don't feel well," I tried whining at my mother over breakfast.

"You feel fine," Mom said.

It's hard to argue with a mother when she's that sure about something. I looked pitifully at my father, but he just smiled.

"Courage, Dana," he said. "You can handle it."

Jean had left early for school, not that I was expecting any words of comfort from her. And even McKitten, who had slept on my bed all night long except for a brief five-A.M. frolic on my face, was more interested in chasing a spool of thread all around the kitchen than in reassuring me. Like it or not (and I sure didn't), this morning I was on my own.

"Have a nice day," Mom called out after me, as I left the house for school. It was shocking to have a mother who was that insensitive.

I walked the longest way I knew to school, and stopped at a lot of different places to look at the way the leaves were changing colors. Things were really very pretty. If I could ever enjoy life again, there would be plenty to enjoy.

I thought I'd dawdled pretty well, but I still got to school way before the first bell was going to ring. I wondered if I could convince my parents to move farther away from the school by the next day. It was a small thing to ask of a mother who said "Have a nice day."

I glanced around the school yard, and didn't like what I saw. Jean was talking with Big Wally and a bunch of her friends, and she obviously wasn't waiting around for me to show up. Sharon was standing in a corner staring down at the ground. And worst of all, Brian was standing at the other end of the school building, instead of being home, suspended, like Charlie had been. The three of them formed a triangle, one I wasn't at all happy about walking into.

Short of running away from home, though, I didn't have a choice. So I gritted my teeth, told myself it couldn't be worse than a graveyard, walked to a spot dead center, then stood still waiting for something to happen.

What did happen surprised me. Sharon walked over and joined me.

"Hi, Dana," she said, almost shyly.

"Sharon?" I said, half suspecting a trick.

"You still mad?" she asked, not quite looking at me.

"I don't know," I said. "Should I be?"

"Maybe," she said. "Look, I thought a lot about what you said yesterday. About how I'm not a very good friend."

"I'm sorry I said all that," I said. "Your advice isn't crappy. It just isn't always right for me."

"Sometimes it's pretty crappy, too," Sharon said. "But I only give it because I care. And because I like giving advice so much."

"I give you advice, too," I said. "Remember that time I told you to wear that red shirt to Jerry Mulligan's party?"

"And everybody told me I looked like a fire hydrant," Sharon said, but she giggled. "Great advice, Dana."

"So I'm not perfect," I said, joining her giggles. It felt so good to be laughing with somebody again.

"I haven't been a very good friend," Sharon said. "Not lately anyway. I guess I've been a little jealous of you, all the attention and everything, and you have done some stuff I thought was kind of dumb, and I really was worried your parents would tell on me to my mother, only they didn't, and I know they won't. Even if they did, I didn't do anything too bad. I just sort of cooperated."

"And gave me advice," I said.

"I didn't make you take it," Sharon said. "So can we be friends again?"

"Sure," I said, and there we were, hugging in the school yard again.

"Look at that!" I heard Charlie call out. "The lovebirds are at it again!"

"Oh, no," Sharon groaned. "It's back."

"Ignore him," I said. "Maybe he'll go away."

So we ignored him, and it actually worked. Charlie sneered in our general direction, but he walked straight over to Brian. All the kids in the school yard followed him with their eyes.

"So you're the guy who set me up!" Charlie said to Brian.

"Maybe," Brian said.

"Nice job," Charlie said, loud enough for all of us to hear. "I would have done it bigger maybe, but you did okay."

Brian stared at him. "You don't mind?" he asked.

"Of course I mind," Charlie said. "I'm going to hit you so hard your mama won't recognize you. You crazy? You think I like being suspended when I'm not even guilty? You know the beating my old man gave me? Nothing compared to what I'm going to do to you."

"I'm sorry," Brian whimpered. "Really, Charlie, I'm sorry. I forgot they were your initials. I thought I was at my old school. There was a kid there . . . Carl Emerson, see, C. E., just like you, and he was a real creep. Nothing like you. And I was putting his initials on the wall, not yours. Honest."

"You give me a pain," Charlie said. "Anybody here believe that garbage?"

We were all silent.

"Good thing," Charlie said. "Anybody sides with this creep is going to end up with a couple of broken arms."

"Then you're going to have to start with mine," I called out.

"Dana!" Sharon gasped.

"Well, I'm sorry, but I'm sick of all this," I said, and walked straight over to Charlie and Brian. "You listen to me, Charlie Everest," I said, not at all sure where all this courage was coming from, but knowing it was mine. "You're a big bully, and nobody likes you, and we've all let you get away with it, but not any longer."

"Who's going to stop me?" he asked with a sneer.

"I will," I said. "I'm braver than you are, Charlie, and I'll stop you."

"You're just a girl," Charlie said.

"That isn't stopping me from telling you off," I said. "But you're right. I can't just stop you alone."

"That's better," Charlie said. "I'd hate to beat up a girl, even an ugly one like you."

"Brian's going to stop you too," I said, hoping Brian would know enough to keep his mouth shut.

"Brian," Charlie snorted. "Don't make me laugh."

"Brian came awfully close to getting you suspended forever, Charlie," I said. "Are you too stupid to see that Brian is mean? He may not be strong and he may not be brave, but he's mean and sneaky, and he's going to do things to you you won't even know are happening. Aren't you, Brian?"

Brian just smiled.

"So you're brave," Charlie said. "And Brian is mean. That's just two of you against me."

"Three of us," Sharon said, walking over to my side.

"I'm sick and tired of your picking on me, Charlie, and I'm not going to take it anymore."

"Well, now I really am scared," Charlie said. "Boy oh boy, I wish my mommy was here to protect me."

"She'll have to protect you from me too," Jean said. "Because if you lay a hand on my sister or any of her friends, you'll have to answer to me."

"I don't even know who you are," Charlie said. "How am I supposed to answer to you?"

"I'm Dana's sister," Jean said, and she put her arm around my shoulder.

"That's real impressive," Charlie said. "Okay, let me get this straight. If I should maybe disturb your sister or any of her little friends, you're going to get mad at me."

"You got it," Jean said.

"I'm wetting my pants," Charlie said. "You guys are a real scream."

"I'm glad they all scared you," Big Wally said, joining us. "That way maybe I won't have to."

Charlie had to crane his neck to make eye contact. Until I saw him standing by Big Wally, I'd never realized just how small Charlie was.

"Who are you?" Charlie squeaked.

"I'm Big Wally," Big Wally replied. "And you'd better remember it, shrimp."

"Don't get him mad," Jean said, smiling up at Big Wally. "He's a monster when he's mad."

"And I always get mad when I see an idiot like you making my friends unhappy," Big Wally said. He stretched one of his arms around Jean, me, Sharon, and Brian. We all managed to crowd in under his grip. "And believe me, punk, you won't want to see me mad."

"Yeah?" Charlie said. "Well, you won't be around all the time to protect them."

"We won't need Big Wally's protection all the time," I said. "If five of us are willing to stand up to you, other kids will be too. You won't know what hit you."

"Okay already," Charlie said. "I get your point."

"You'd better not forget it, too," Big Wally said. "Because I'm going to be keeping an eye on you, squirt. And don't you ever forget it."

"I won't, I won't." Charlie said. "Now, if you don't mind, I'd like to go to school. Alone. If it's okay with all of you."

"Sure," Sharon said. "This time."

"Jeez," Charlie said, but he walked into the school building without another look at us.

"That was fun," Jean said. "Big Wally, that was so sweet of you." She squeezed his hand, and that let us all break away from his embrace.

"It's okay," Big Wally said. "I don't like to see little kids get picked on."

"Thanks, Big Wally," I said. "And thank you, Jean."

"Well, you are my sister," she said. "Besides, if Charlie picked on you all the time, you'd always be center of attention. And I couldn't stand that." She gave Brian, Sharon, and me a victory sign and walked into the school building hand in hand with Big Wally.

"I don't understand," Brian said. "Why didn't you just tell Charlie that you were the one who got him back into school? He never would have laid a hand on you again. How come you stuck up for me instead?"

"Because I hate Charlie," I said. "And I don't hate you."

"Oh," Brian said. "Oh." He looked me over for a moment and then put his hand out. "Friends?" he asked.

I put my hand out too and smiled at him as we shook. Brian smiled back, and then walked into the school with his shoulders thrown back and a real grin on his face.

"Wow," Sharon said. "That was really something, Dana."

"Yeah, I guess it was," I said. "I didn't even think. I just got so sick of Charlie."

"That's real bravery," Sharon said. "I'll never call you a coward again."

I glanced at her and knew she would. We were still best friends, but that didn't mean she was always going to think as highly of me as she did just then. We'd insulted each other and fought and made up much too often for me to expect that to stop.

"I think I'm going to take a course in CPR," I told her.

"CPR," she said. "What's that?"

"I don't know what it stands for exactly," I said, and we started walking toward the school steps. "But it teaches you what to do in case somebody has a heart attack. You know, you're walking down the street and some strange guy collapses in front of you because he's had a heart attack, and you've had CPR so you bend over and breathe into his mouth and save his life."

"That's the craziest thing I've ever heard," Sharon said, and we started up the steps. "You breathe into some strange guy's mouth? What if he has a disease?"

"But that isn't why he collapsed," I said. "He had a heart attack and that isn't catching."

"It sounds awfully weird to me," Sharon said. "Still, he might be a rich person and he'd be grateful if you saved his life."

"Grateful enough for a four-year scholarship?" I asked.

"It's worth a try," Sharon said. "Maybe I'll take the course with you. No reason why you should be the heroine all the time."

"No reason at all," I said. "Come on, Sharon, we're going to be late."

"Maybe med school, too," Sharon said, and she skipped up the last couple of steps. "Can you imagine? A free medical education just because you breathed the right way into some guy's mouth."

"You might only get a free book," I told her.

"It's worth the risk," she said. "I'll do it if you will."

"You're on," I said, and, holding the door open, we walked in together.

Bestselling books by

Beverly Cleary